The Outpost

Cameron Black figured he was due for some luck. With a posse on his trail and the desert crawling with hostile Indians he finally managed to make it to the isolated army outpost. The trouble was the post was manned only by a skeleton crew of weary soldiers, among them three would-be deserters waiting for a chance to steal the army payroll.

Also trapped inside by circumstances were a US marshal who Black had known on the backtrail, his young prisoner and a group of female camp-followers. Among them was Cameron's old-time lover.

Even with the Comanches gearing up to attack the outpost, Cameron felt like making a dash across the desert, because there was nothing here but certain trouble.

The Outpost

Owen G. Irons

A Black Horse Western

ROBERT HALE · LONDON

ISBN 978-0-7090-8715-1

Robert Hale Limited
Clerkenwell House
Clerkenwell Green
London EC1R 0HT

www.halebooks.com

Typeset by
Derek Doyle & Associates, Shaw Heath
Printed and bound in Great Britain by
CPI Antony Rowe, Chippenham and Eastbourne

ONE

The New Mexico plain was flat, black, cold and devoid of vegetation except for scattered sage and greasewood. Night had fallen hours earlier, but the riders dared not stop. The rumor of a Comanche uprising had been confirmed by their discovery at the burned-out stage station back at Piccolo: six men and a woman savagely killed, their bodies mutilated. The two men carried the burden of fear with them as their struggling horses plodded on toward the outpost garrisoned by 3rd Cavalry soldiers. There they could find a measure of comfort and safety from the hostiles.

The lead rider was named John Macafee. Big John, they had called him in his younger days, but now time had eroded some of the muscular flesh of youth from his bones. He was tall, angular, lanky, wearing a white mustache drooping into points. His eyes were hard and cold blue. He had seen much trouble in his time as a law officer, but had reached the point in his life when he just wanted to survive long enough to die a natural death.

The man riding with him had already decided that a natural death was not to be his fate. At nineteen years of age Brian Tyson was a murderer, and his life would be ended quite legally when the hangman in Socorro fitted him with the noose. Brian was not so much afraid as disoriented, disembodied almost, a man observing, but not understanding his own slow, descending journey toward perdition. There was even a time, back at the ruined way-station as they buried the dead, that Brian Tyson almost wished he was among them. That way it would have been all over. No more concerns, no more fear, just the dark sleep that faded into eternity.

Now he sat his patiently plodding buckskin horse, his manacled hands resting on the pommel of his saddle. Fifty feet of loose rope was knotted around the pommel, the other end tied to

Macafee's saddlehorn. The old man had not been cruel to Brian, had in fact been kind, but in the sternest manner.

'Boy,' the mustached marshal had warned Brian, 'I am going to take you in. Now it's up to you how much energy I have to expend in doing so. I warn you, if you make me expend too much, it will go hard on you. If it goes hard enough for long enough, I'll just plug you and tie you across the saddle. It all pays the same.'

Brian knew the lawman meant it. He hadn't offered any resistance. What was the point in it, anyway? Someone else would just come after him, and then someone else. There was no sense in struggling against the currents of justice. He had killed a man; he must now pay for it.

'There it is,' Brian heard Macafee say in that dry tone of his. He was not speaking directly to Brian Tyson, but as a man will when there are ears around to hear his thoughts. Lifting his eyes, Brian saw the rising, serrated palisade of the outpost. Backlighted by the pale coming half-moon, the sharpened stakes resembled dragons' teeth, dark and threatening. Brian saw no lanternlight, heard no sounds emanating from the fort.

'Quiet, isn't it?' he asked.

7

'It's past midnight, boy,' Macafee said, as if it were logical, but Brian wondered. Surely a strong guard would be posted after the news of the Comanche uprising reached the fort.

The night seemed to hover over them, still, star-bright but menacing in an undefined way. The weary horses dragged their hoofs as they proceeded across the red sand desert. The scent of sage and creosote was heavy in the air although the brush grew only in widely scattered clumps. Brian had no liking for the feelings crowding his mind. But then, he reflected with a mental shrug, death holds little fear for a man who is already as good as dead.

They drew their exhausted horses up in front of the twenty-foot high double gates to the outpost and Marshal Macafee called out. His voice was hoarse and faint at first, but grew louder and more demanding as his calls went unanswered.

'Got to be someone standing guard,' he muttered angrily, and sang out again: 'Hello the fort!'

Brian sat shivering in the darkness; the night had grown cold across the desert. Macafee had started to swing down from his pony when the Judas gate set into the tall palisades swung open on rusty iron hinges.

'Who goes there?' an almost deferential voice called.

'Marshal John Macafee out of Socorro, and a prisoner. We require refuge for the night.'

There was no response. The Judas gate closed. A bolt was thrown. After another long minute one of the two great gates to the outpost was swung open and, frowning, Macafee rode into the dark compound, leading Brian.

The gate was closed behind them, a bar dropped across its face. The man who had come to meet them returned to stand before Macafee's horse. He wore a half-smile. His face was as pale as ivory, his eyes deep-set. He wore an unbuttoned army tunic and was hatless.

'Have any trouble out there?' the apparition asked.

'Not personally, but we came across a massacre back to Piccolo. What's the army doing about this?'

'The best we can,' their host answered. 'The colonel and most of the regiment rode out six days ago, trying to track the renegades. A tougher job than they imagined, it seems. Only five of us were left behind to stand watch over the post, in the hope that the Comanches wouldn't figure out how undermanned we are.'

'Where are the other troopers?' Macafee wondered aloud. 'Sleeping at a time like this?'

'Don't know,' the ghostly trooper answered. 'They took off a couple, three days ago. Most of these young boys are only here for the steady pay, a lot of them were given the choice between joining the army or doing prison time – hard as it is to keep our ranks up to quota the way the country's expanding. They never actually considered what having to fight a bunch of angry Comanches might mean. At the first sign of trouble, they deserted. No surprise; it happens all the time.'

'So, who,' Macafee who had now dismounted, asked, 'remains here? Surely you're not alone.'

'No. Lieutenant Young is here and his wife – they couldn't leave. She's been in child labor for nearly two days. There's them and the ladies,' the trooper said, as if the term was not one of respect. 'Come along, Marshal. You'll at least have water and fodder for your ponies. The place is dark because we have little wood left and but a few ounces of kerosene for our lanterns. If the colonel doesn't get back soon – if he can – we'll be on starvation rations. But I suppose this still beats being out in the desert.'

The man leaped for his saddled gray horse as the first shots were fired, two of them, both missing wildly. From their report and the cloud of rising black smoke each issued, he figured the weapons for ancient muskets, unreliable and inaccurate. The other weapons they carried were even more ancient, but truer. An arrow whipped past his head as he ducked and ran, leaving his coffee pot and saddle-bags beside the small, faintly flickering fire he had been crouched over in the arroyo. The first arrow buried its head in the fire, the second struck the big gray gelding in the hip and it leaped, crow-hopped and kicked its hind legs, futilely trying to dislodge it.

The man snatched at the trailing reins of the big horse and with difficulty grabbed them up, mounting the horse on the run as two more ill-aimed shots from the muzzle-loaders were fired behind him. He cursed the loss of his saddle-bags – but let the renegades have them if that was all this night cost him. Nothing in them was worth his life.

He seldom used his spurs, but now he dug them

into the gray's flanks. He could feel the animal falter under him. Ordinarily the big horse would have no trouble at all outdistancing the scraggly Indian ponies the Comanches rode, but now the animal was virtually running on three legs, and there was no time to halt and see to the arrow wound.

But after an initial chorus of derisive yells, there were no war cries, and no sign of pursuit. The night was dark, the land long, and they had realized that they had nothing to gain by a long pursuit. Gradually the man slowed the big animal which was frothing at the mouth, angry and in obvious pain.

What now? Camping alone, far from prying eyes had always been a part of his pattern. The now unsettled situation on the plains called for a different strategy. He could have as easily been struck in the skull by a musket ball as he slept. Some sort of defensible position was needed. He seemed to recall that an army outpost had been planned along the Lower Pecos. If they had completed that fort, he could shelter up there, and if not too many questions were asked, feel secure for a while at least.

There was little choice, really. The gray, faltering

12

and unable to run, could not carry him much further. Slowing the wounded animal to a walk, he turned its head toward where he believed the outpost stood.

Coldly dark, the night ran on. He rode through a scattering of pines and live oak trees until, emerging into full moonlight he saw the outpost, small and defiant. There were no trees near the fort; they had been cleared long ago with the dual purpose of using them to construct the outpost and leaving lines of fire open. He saw no one on the ramparts. The flag, of course, was not flying this long after sundown. He hesitated, stroking his anxious gray horse's neck. There were too many people he did not wish to meet again, and he had never had good luck in his dealings with the army.

Approaching the outpost carefully, his eyes searched for life; found none. If it were not for the muffled blowing of a horse within the stockade, he would have taken it for a deserted structure. But the horse nickered and his wounded pony answered and, sighing inwardly, the weary man started on toward the fort.

'Who goes there?' a weak voice answered after his third hail.

Unwilling to shout his real name, the man called back, 'Only a lonely wanderer, friend,' and after another long interval the gate was swung open, letting his limping horse straggle into the interior of the fort. Swinging down as soon as the gate was shut behind him, he waited for the sentry to return. A narrow, tired-appearing man, his face waxen in the lantern light, shuffled to meet him.

'Let me have that lantern,' the younger, taller man said.

Holding it higher he was able to see the arrow which still protruded from the gray's flank. The man's mouth tightened. He said, 'Damnit – looks like I'll have to cut it out of there.'

'How many jumped you?' the small man in the army-blue tunic asked.

'No more than five or six. They weren't well-armed, as you can tell by this,' he replied, indicating the arrow shaft.

'I guess they'd give a lot to bust our armory open, wouldn't they?'

'Well, sure! But you must have enough troopers here to prevent something like that from happening.'

The old soldier looked at the tall, unshaven,

14

dark-haired man and attempted a smile. 'You'd think we would, wouldn't you? But we're kind of what you might call in dire straits here, stranger. Let's go over to the stable and you can see to your horse. I'll tell you our situation along the way.'

The cutting was the hardest part. The flint arrowhead had penetrated a good six inches into the horse's rump. There was no way to calm the horse or explain what they were trying to do. At the first incision made with the man's razor-edged skinning knife, the gray began to buck and kick, tossing its head wildly. Although it took only a minute, the gray remained resentful and wild-eyed as they poured carbolic over the wound and tried – unsuccessfully – to soothe it.

'He'll be all right come morning,' the soldier said. By the dim light of the lantern, the man now saw that he wore corporal's stripes. He had introduced himself as Demarest. It was clear that the man was ill. Possibly with tuberculosis. Flaccid and unsteady, it was obvious why Demarest had been left behind to stand guard duty rather than asked to ride with the company of troopers pursuing the renegade Comanche Indians.

Now breathless and unnerved, he said to the

15

newcomer, 'Best come along now and meet the others.' Stepping outside of the stable into the cold desert night, they heard a screaming complaint against the forces of life and death. A terrible, keening sound. The man looked to Demarest for an explanation.

'The lieutenant's wife. She's a small thing and this is her first birthing. We think the kid's turned the wrong way.' He shook his head. 'It's a terrible, terrible thing. She's so young and the lieutenant is about to go out of his mind with worry.'

'I see,' the stranger said. There was nothing else to say. The agonized cry seemed to echo in the air for minutes. Worst of all, as both men knew, even if the woman survived, if the baby was born healthy, the savages beyond the palisades were capable of making new life end as painfully as it had begun.

'Any idea what set the renegades off?' the man asked.

'No one does. There's been a few guesses, but I suppose we'll never know for sure.' Demarest panted as he tried to speak. The ageing corporal was in no shape for this duty, for any fight. How he had ended up stranded on the New Mexico desert at this time of life, without future expectations, was a matter of speculation, but there were so many possibilities that delving deeper was pointless.

'Here is where they're all holed up,' Demarest said. He lifted the lantern slightly so that the face of a low log building was vaguely illuminated. 'Used to be a ballroom in the days when the officers and their wives would hold dances. In the back are a few rooms where visiting civilians were billeted. You saw the stable – that small cubbyhole was the smith's work area. That there is the bachelor officers' quarters. No one there now. Then there's the headquarters building – right over there, you can almost see it. Colonel's office and a room to one side for the first sergeant. The long building, of course, is the barracks. There used to be a sutler's store to your left, but the man running it couldn't get any supplies in here after the insurrection started, and he hitched his mules and scatted for Alamosa months ago. Smart man,' Corporal Demarest said ruefully.

'Who's here now?' the man asked cautiously, as they reached the steps of the large building Demarest had identified as a 'ballroom'. Low lights burned within and there were muted sounds of conversation.

'Altogether? Me, Lieutenant Young and his wife.

17

Some lawman named Macafee who's escorting a murderer to Socorro. And the women.'

'The women?' the man asked with a frown.

'Yes, sir. They sort of got stranded here . . .' Demarest paused, sorting through his thoughts, trying to find the best way to put it. 'In my day, in the War, they used to call them camp-followers. Maybe they still do. They used to come by in their wagon every month on payday. Well, this time when they showed up, it was the day we went on full alert and Colonel Hayes, he was in no mood to talk to or listen to anybody. The troops were mounted, and the women were ordered to stay in the outpost. Oh, they complained, but they saw that the colonel was dead serious, and so they stayed put. They have been helpful with the cooking and such, and with trying to comfort Mrs Young. Otherwise . . . well, frankly, I just wish they weren't here, if you know what I mean. Not right now. I don't wish to see them . . . hurt.'

They had stamped up onto the porch and Corporal Demarest swung the door to. The victims of circumstance were about to meet each other.

*

Entering the broad hall, its interior lighted only dimly by scattered smoky light, they found the small assemblage somewhere in between wide-eyed fear and exhaustion. No one slept, but all seemed in need of it.

'This here is Marshal Macafee,' Demarest said, flipping a hand toward the lean, blue-eyed man who sat at a round table with a young, desperate-looking companion. 'And his prisoner – I didn't catch your name, young fellow.'

'Brian Tyson,' he responded dully. Eyeing the two, the man saw that Tyson had his right arm beneath the table, and he guessed that the hand was manacled to the table leg. He only nodded to the men. It was Macafee who spoke.

'Haven't I seen you before? Maybe down Taos way?'

'Never been there,' the man lied. The lawman's eyes narrowed and followed the two as they crossed the ballroom to where three women sat awaiting their approach. One of them, quite young and pretty wore yellow satin, a second, plainer and darker, was dressed in red. The older woman wore deep blue, had her hair neatly pinned and wore a sardonic smile. She was dealing out a hand of soli-taire from a well-used deck of cards. Her dark eyes

19

registered surprise, welcome and disbelief at once.

'Hello,' she said.

'Hello, Scopes,' he answered. He removed his hat as he nodded to the three women.

'You two know each other?' Demarest asked in confusion.

'In passing,' Virginia Scopes replied, squaring the deck of blue-backed cards in her hand. The diamond rings on her fingers sparkled with reflected fire.

Demarest scratched at his ear and said, 'Well . . . I guess I'll leave you alone for now. I haven't had any sleep for two days.'

His speech was interrupted by yet another agonized scream from across the parade ground. It was a chilling cry, pleading to God and the universe for relief from pain. The man remained standing, but when Corporal Demarest had turned away and departed, he sat beside Virginia Scopes and asked, 'Can't something be done for that woman?'

'No,' the lady in blue said, turning up a black five to play on a red six. 'It's a breech birth – you know what that is? Without a real doctor, it's a matter of time, a matter of life and death for her and the baby.'

'The lieutenant – Young, is it? – must be going out of his mind.'

'He should have left her alone then!' Virginia said sharply, unreasonably. Considering her current profession, it seemed a naïve remark as well.

Taking a deep breath, flipping over a jack which matched nothing on the board, she asked, 'How goes it, Cam?'

'All right, I suppose.' He glanced at the two anxious nearby girls who were too distracted to have overheard his name being spoken. The marshal, far across the room, continued to watch them suspiciously, but could have heard nothing either. 'I'm just trying to get out of the territory. The Comanches are the least of my worries. I've a few well-meaning, mistaken citizens on my trail.'

'As usual,' Virginia Scopes said with a sigh that lifted her bosom high. She slapped the deck of cards down and gazed intently into Cameron Black's eyes. 'When are you going to quit trying to make a living with that gun of yours?'

Cameron seemed to seriously consider the question for a long minute before he answered with a sardonic grin: 'When it stops paying so well! Men want me; they pay me to take care of their

21

problems.' He added, 'I guess I'll stop about the same time you give up your business – when the men no longer need us or we're just too damned old to ply our trade.'

'Thanks,' Virginia muttered.

'I didn't mean anything by it, Scopes.'

'I know it.' Her hand rested briefly on his, then withdrew quickly. A gesture reflecting the old days which was no longer fitting. Too many trails had divided them. Youth had flown away. They had been lovers; now they were just an ageing gunfighter and a whore.

Virginia introduced the other two women. Cameron rose and took their soft hands gingerly as if they could be easily crushed.

'This is Squeaky,' Virginia said, indicating the very young blonde in yellow satin. Her lip trembled anxiously. There was trouble etched deeply into her blue eyes. 'And Kate.' The slightly older girl was a brunette stuffed tightly into a flounced red dress. Her dark eyes reflected only resignation. Perhaps she had already decided that her life was over, doomed before it had begun.

Cameron Black nodded and murmured a few unmeant and unheard words to each of the ladies. Three shots from outside the fort slashed across the relative silence and spurred each of them to motion.

Reflexively Cam slicked his .44 Colt from its holster in a quick, fluid motion that did not escape the eyes of Marshal Macafee. The lawman was also rising to his feet. Brian Tyson, manacled to the table leg struggled to respond but could not. The front door to the ballroom burst open and a young, wild-eyed army officer burst in, holding his .45–70 Springfield rifle. Hatless and disheveled, he looked like a man who had devils riding his coat-tails.

Lieutenant Young shouted out, 'To the walls, boys!' as if he had a body of men to respond to his order. Cameron Black started that way as did Macafee. Beyond, they could see Corporal Demarest struggling up the ladder leading to the parapet, lantern in hand. His long, wavering shadow stretched out across the hard-packed parade ground and slithered up the rungs of the ladder as he moved.

From the corner of his eye Cameron Black saw the young prisoner – Brian Tyson hoist the table and slip his manacle beneath its leg. Tyson started off at a wild run and Cameron tripped him as he passed, sending the kid sprawling.

'Damn you,' Brian shouted, his eyes blazing with anger. 'I could have made it!'

'Out on the desert crawling with Comanches, without a horse?' Cameron said coldly. 'You'd just have found a way to shorten your life even more. This way, there may be a chance for you.'

Brian Tyson continued to curse in muffled tones. He sleeved blood away from his bleeding nose and sat up, arms wrapped around his knees, still glaring at Cameron Black.

Outside, the lantern on the ramparts swung vigorously from side to side and Demarest cupped a hand to his mouth and called down, 'It's Hazzard and his men. They've come back!'

Standing beside the young lieutenant on the porch, Marshal Macafee asked, 'Who is Hazzard?'

'Deserters,' Lieutenant Young answered tightly. 'I suppose they couldn't get past the renegades.' To Demarest, Young called wearily, 'All right, Corporal, let them in! God knows what I'm to do with them. They outnumber us! I'll leave it to the colonel to decide when he gets back . . . if he gets back,' he added dismally.

The gates swung open heavily and the returning deserters walked their weary horses into the outpost. From across the open ground the woman again screamed in the agony of troubled child-birth.

Cameron Black glanced at the incoming riders, at Marshal Macafee and his prisoner, and met the eyes of Virginia Scopes. And he wondered if he might not have been wiser to take his chances out on the desert than dealing with those inside the fort.

TWO

The howling chants began around midnight, ululating sounds which might have come from the throats of coyotes, but were in fact the war songs of the Comanche renegades.

'They're damnably close,' Lieutenant Young said, running his hands through his hair. His eyes were feverish with excitement. He was on the verge of losing his young wife and child and his command at once. It was a lot for a man to bear. 'We need someone to stand watch from the ramparts,' he said, looking around at the small group. Hazzard and his two fellow deserters were there in the ballroom, looking haggard and weary. The fourth member of their party, they revealed, had been taken down by the Comanches and chopped to hash.

Besides them there was only the marshal who was loath to leave his prisoner unguarded and the other man – Young hadn't gotten his name; it hadn't been offered. He eyed Cameron Black now, noting the rangy form of the man, the two guns. The stag-handled Colt revolvers rode on either hip, but both were arranged for a right-handed draw. The butt of the left-hand gun facing forward for a cross-draw. He had dark, slightly wavy hair, prominent cheekbones and eyes with crows' feet lines cornering them, from harsh weather and sun, or perhaps from smiling frequently, but Young saw no indication that the man was given to frequent amusement.

'I'll stand watch for awhile,' Cameron Black volunteered, rising from his seat beside Virginia. 'I'd like to have a long gun, if you don't mind.'

The lieutenant hesitated and then handed over the .45–70 army-issue rifle he had been carrying loosely in his hand. He added a handful of cartridges and nodded his thanks to the tall man.

Again from across the parade ground came the cry of a woman in deep distress and Lieutenant Young bowed his head as if his anguish made it impossible to hold it high. Virginia Scopes rose, smoothing her skirts and said, 'I'll go sit with

Mattie for a while if you like, Lieutenant. You look as if you could use a few hours' rest.'

'Yes, yes – thank you,' Young said wearily. He seemed unable or unwilling to bear all that had been heaped upon his shoulders. He glanced at Hazzard and his cohorts and murmured, 'I'll talk to you later. I'm sure the colonel will be interested to hear what you have to say when he returns.'

Hazzard, a bullish man still wearing his unbuttoned army tunic, smirked as he answered, 'All right, sir. As you wish.' His two companions were too weary to laugh, but each formed a small smile, knowing that Lieutenant Young had no power over them now.

One of them, a skinny blond man they had called Harding, rose, stretched and sidled toward the back of the room to seat himself on the bench beside Kate, the dark woman in the red dress. He whispered something into her ear and she blushed, looked briefly shocked and then laughed.

'Pigs they are,' Marshal Macafee said to Brian Tyson who watched all of the by-play distantly. None of it could affect his own sharply attenuated life. People would flirt. Men would challenge one another. Women might die. Life would go on until mortality claimed them all. He would simply hang by the neck until dead in Socorro.

'Pigs who would desert their post in time of war,' Macafee said more loudly, and this time Hazzard seemed to hear him. His porcine eyes shifted toward the lawman and his prisoner.

'Funny, isn't it,' Hazzard said to his companion, a balding man with his trooper's cap shoved back off his brow, 'people that never been in a situation think they know everything about it. Isn't that the way it always goes, Jason?' The other man only shrugged. He looked uncomfortable. Hazzard's eyes locked with Marshal Macafee's. 'Yes, that's the way it always goes. Those who know the least about a situation are the first to speak up about it.'

Then, before Macafee could muster a response, Hazzard rose and said to Jason, 'Let's go over to the barracks. I need some shuteye. Harding! Are you coming with us?'

The younger trooper hesitated, but he rose, still holding on to the brunette's hand, and answered, 'I'm on my way.' Nodding to the women, he touched his hat briefly and strode toward the door, swaggering as if he had no concerns at all about the trouble beyond the gates. The two women – Squeaky and Kate – put their heads together and whispered excitedly. Something was in the works,

Macafee knew, but he had no idea what it might be beyond the obvious.

'Pigs, I'm telling you,' Macafee grumbled again. He rose heavily and walked to the iron stove in the corner where a poor vegetable soup simmered in a black iron pot and coffee boiled. He poured himself a cup of the coffee and one for the prisoner and started back toward the table.

Sullenly he sat and sipped the dark, bitter coffee. Periodically they heard rifle shots fired from the rampart beyond. The reports seemed to get on Brian Tyson's nerves. Finally he said, 'What the hell is he doing? Shooting at ghosts and shadows? He can't possibly see anything out there!'

'That's exactly what he's doing,' Big John Macafee answered. 'Shooting at ghosts and shadows. He can't see the Comanches, but they don't know that – and it gives them something to think about. Whoever the man is, he knows something about Indian fighting.'

'He looks like a gunfighter to me,' Brian Tyson said, lifting his cup unsteadily to his lips. 'The way he carries those guns of his.'

'Could be, could be,' answered Macafee, who had reached the same conclusion. 'And we're better off for having him around if that's the case.'

'You could take these manacles off and give me a gun,' Brian said out of desperation. 'I could be a help.'

'Yes, son,' Macafee said carefully, 'or I could just cut my own throat.' After another minute, he asked quietly, 'Why *did* you kill that man, Tyson?'

'Why!' Brian throttled a laugh. His free hand was wrapped tightly around his tin coffee cup. He seemed briefly on the edge of hysterics, but calmed himself and explained as simply as he could.

'I was riding fence down on the Anchor Ranch. About nooning, I started back toward the big house to get my grub. Old man Gere who owned the Anchor had four daughters, widely spaced. The youngest was a slender girl named Emma – she was all of fourteen years old when the men started to notice her. Gere gathered all of us in the bunkhouse one day to let us know that he would hang any man who laid a hand on her.

'Well, on this particular day I was riding down a sandy wash when I came upon a new-hired hand named Wallace. He was tangled up in a stand of sumac with a bunch of blue calico and a pair of white legs and the girl was crying, just crying her heart out. . . .

31

'I shot him dead in cold blood.'

Macafee was silent. 'Didn't Gere, the girl – someone – come forward and tell the judge that it was
justifiable homicide?'

'No one spoke for me,' Brian Tyson said. 'Gere
didn't want to put his daughter through interroga-
tion. He didn't even show up at the hearing. I
managed to break out of jail and I took off on my
pony for the mountains, but they caught me pretty
quick. They said that my running away was as good
as an admission of guilt. That's what happened,
Macafee. I guess I murdered the man. I mean, I *did*
do it! But it seemed at the time. . . .'

His voice faded away and Macafee asked no
more questions. From the rampart Cameron Black
fired another shot. The Comanches had not given
up yet.

Cameron reloaded the Springfield breech-loader
and marched lazily along the rampart, careful to
keep his head below the sharpened stakes of the
palisade. The Indians, he decided, were waiting for
more of their clan to gather. Once they had determined how thin the garrison was, they would
come. The armory, of course, was their prime
objective, but horses, supplies, possibly a few blue-

back scalps to revenge past defeats would also be motivation for an assault.

At each end of the parapet was a rough-hewn wooden bench, and now after firing another aimless shot into the distances, Cameron seated himself on one of these. The shot was a futile gesture, really; nevertheless it might give the renegades pause for thought.

The half moon rose higher into the clear, starry sky. A desert coyote yipped. The night was cold and empty. He thought first and primarily of a way to protect those inside the outpost, but gradually, inexorably, his mind drifted to Virginia Scopes. What a place, such circumstances to run into her again!

Time runs past, flowing more quickly than any mountain stream, yet unlike a river its rapid course is not swift enough to sweep away memories. Whose fault it had been, Cameron was no longer sure. He had always placed the blame squarely in Virginia's lap. That, he supposed was only human nature. But now, looking back, he could see a little of how she had perceived him: a young Cameron Black, cocky and assertive, intent on making his way through the world with his Colt revolvers. Not exactly an attractive type for a young Colorado farm girl to put her faith and trust in.

Initially she had seemed attracted by his rough-shod image, and Cameron had gone out of his way to embellish it. After a series of bloody skirmishes, however, she had come to hate the violent side of him. The only thing was, he knew no other life. Even had he been able to give it up for her, some-one would come hunting for him sooner or later. Someone always did.

Even now a group of citizens from Victorville was looking for him. He had given the man a fair chance in the fight, but what chance did the sodbuster really have against Cameron Black in a gunfight? Black had been hired for the job by a man named Norman, but Norman had not pulled the trigger on that hot, dusty day: Cameron Black had.

Cameron, feeling quite old at that moment, rose, lethargically fired two shots into the trees beyond the fort and seated himself again.

And Virginia? How had she become what she was now? And whose fault was that? He shook his head heavily and stared at his bloodstained hands.

'Coming up!' Corporal Demarest called up in warning from the foot of the ladder. Reaching Black he said, 'I'll stand watch for awhile. I got a couple of hours of sleep, and it seems you could use some.'

'Thanks,' Cameron nodded, handing over the rifle and cartridges Lieutenant Young had given him. 'How's the girl doing?'

'No change,' Demarest said. 'Looks like that baby just doesn't want to come into this world.'

'Can't blame it much, can you?' Cameron muttered.

'I guess not,' Demarest agreed dismally. 'No, I guess you can't.'

THREE

Cameron descended the rampart ladder by moonlight. He stood surveying the fort for a long moment. The ballroom had been uncomfortable, infinitely depressing in an ill-defined way. He needed rest but did not wish to go to the enlisted men's barracks where the three deserters were presumably sleeping. A part of him tugged him toward where the BOQ – base officers' quarters – were located, knowing that Virginia Scopes was sitting up with the suffering Mattie Long, but he did not feel that he could face Virginia again, not so soon. And he could be of no possible help to the young army wife.

He shifted his guns into a more comfortable position and walked beneath the moonlit, starry sky toward the stables. Even his horse, he reflected, was bound to be angry with him for the cruel cut of his knife. It seemed at that moment that everything Cameron Black had tried to accomplish in his life ended up with negative, unintended results. After briefly checking his nervous gray horse which refused to be calmed, Cameron climbed the pole ladder to the hayloft where he strewed some loose straw around and stretched out for an uncomfortable, but necessary rest. He wasted only a few hours remembering the younger Virginia Scopes and Cameron Black.

What awoke him in the early morning hours, he could not have said. Coyotes yipping, rats scuttling through the hay, but once awake he rose in the chill of the pre-dawn hours and stiffly made his way down the ladder to the stable floor.

Outside the building, the moon still dreamed in the silky sky, but was descending rapidly. There was enough starlight to see yet, and by it, Cameron saw the shadowy figure of a man slipping silently past the headquarters building. Frowning, he resettled his hat and started that way. He caught only a glimpse of the shadowy figure as it paused beside the single window on the western side of the building and vanished into the night. A silent intruder, he made no sound as he moved. It could not be a

Comanche, Cameron knew, so perhaps a white man wearing moccasins? Shaking his head, he walked on past the building. Although his hand had tensed just above his Colt, he had no thought of firing it. He was a stranger in a strange place and had no idea who the man had been or what he had been doing.

He did, however, have an inkling.

There was a raised boardwalk along the front of the base officers' quarters and, as Cameron stepped onto it and made his way forward, his leather bootheels clicked loudly in the quiet of the night.

The lantern was still lit – the wick turned very low – in Lieutenant Young's residence.

Cameron had raised his hand to knock when he saw that the door stood ajar. He opened the door with his toe and slipped inside. Virginia was there, at Mattie Young's bedside and her head came up in angered fear.

'What are you doing here?' Virginia asked in a hiss. She had removed her blue dress and now wore only her chemise. Her dark hair had been let down and brushed across her shoulders and breast. Cameron hesitated, briefly surprised, like a man who has stumbled into a lady's boudoir accidentally. Virginia was on her feet, and she took Cameron's elbow, guiding him from the room. Behind her a pale, inert Mattie Young lay, hands at her side, perspiration on her forehead and throat.

Virginia eased the door shut, crossed her arms and stood facing Cameron Black on the boardwalk as the starry night ran by.

'I wondered if she was all right,' Cameron answered in a whisper, although Mattie was asleep and she could not have heard them through the solid door.

'For now she is,' Virginia said, her manner softening slightly. 'But the baby inside her will wake up and it will all start over again. The poor little thing just can't find its way out.'

Cameron nodded, knowing but not truly understanding what the young woman must be going though and would continue to endure. Along the rampart someone – probably the sickly Corporal Demarest – stood in stark relief against the starry night.

'At least the Indians have pulled back, or at least delayed,' Cameron commented. 'Where's Lieutenant Young?'

'Asleep in the adjoining room,' Virginia said,

her dark eyes searching his. 'Why? Is something wrong?'

'I think so. I need to talk to him when he's up.'

Virginia used her fingers to comb back her dark hair. It was longer than Cameron remembered it, not so raven-dark as it had once been. The starlight caught a few hints of silver in it. 'Not about the Comanches?' she asked.

'No. There's something else afoot.'

They both fell silent for awhile, standing side by side on the plankwalk, looking at the blur of twinkling stars above.

'What are we doing here?' Virginia asked suddenly, quite softly.

'Right here, right now? Or anywhere on this planet at all?' He expected no answer, received none from the woman at his shoulder.

'If they catch up with you, will they kill you, Cam?'

'They'll give it a try. I think they put a bounty on me this time.' He shook his head with bitter regret at the missteps of his wasted life.

'Do they know how banged up you really are?' Virginia asked, taking him by the shoulders, turning him to face her.

'What are you talking about?' he asked with a

hollow laugh. The woman knew him too well to be deceived.

'The way you're wearing your guns, Cam. You never did that before. You can't draw with your left hand any more, can you? Where did they get you? Shoulder, hand?' He still didn't reply, and she went on with a deepening sadness. 'How many times have you been shot, Cam? Really? Tell me.' Her hands tightened on his shoulders and then fell away as she diverted her eyes.

'I carry a little ballast,' he said lightly. Then his own mood grew more somher. 'It seems that you do too.'

There was a moment when their eyes met, and Virginia's lips parted as if she would speak of other things, but through the door they could make out the murmured sounds of Mattie Young stirring and they parted without another word, Cam striding toward the ballroom, Virginia watching after him for a few long seconds.

The two women in the ballroom were curled up on the floor, covered with Indian blankets. Their dresses were hung carelessly on pegs. Marshal John Macafee was at the iron stove, prodding at the wood in the potbelly. He turned, enamel cup in hand and blinked with surprise.

'Morning,' Macafee said drily.

'It will be soon,' Cameron Black replied, walking to the stove to pour himself a cup of the day-old coffee. 'How are you feeling, Macafee?'

'I'm all right,' the lawman answered with surprise. 'Why do you ask?'

'The old man – Demarest – he's still standing guard. He could use someone to spell him.'

'What makes that my job?' Macafee replied edgily. 'There's other soldiers to relieve him.'

'I don't think they will. I think they've got other plans. I have to talk to Lieutenant Young as soon as possible.'

'You forget I've got a prisoner to see to,' John Macafee said, nodding toward Brian Tyson who still sat at the plank table, handcuffed to the leg, his head resting on his other forearm, quite asleep.

'I'll watch him,' Cameron Black promised. 'I didn't let him make his escape last time, did I? Besides, he has nowhere to go.'

'I don't like this,' Macafee said, scowling.

'I know you don't, but you'll like it a lot less if we get overrun by renegades because Demarest has fallen asleep on duty.'

The two men locked eyes for a moment, measuring each other. Then, with a sigh, Macafee banged his coffee cup down and muttered, 'Oh, hell! OK. I suppose you're right. I'll spell Demarest.' He paused. One of the women stirred under her blankets and both men glanced that way. Marshal Macafee asked quietly, 'You said that you believe something is up. Do you mind telling me what it is?'

'I have to talk to Lieutenant Young first,' Cam answered with a shake of his head. 'I could be wrong. Once the lieutenant's awake, we'll discuss it and let you know.'

'All right,' Macafee said. He swept back his gray hair and put on his wide-brimmed hat. He gave a last warning to Cameron: 'See that you don't let the kid get loose!'

Cameron answered obliquely, 'Is there any more firewood around? Everyone will be waking up soon.'

'From what I understand those few twigs are the last of it,' Macafee replied. 'I don't think they'll be sending out a wood-cutting party anytime soon.'

With that, the scowling marshal stalked from the room, letting one last glance linger on the sleeping, chained prisoner. Unnecessarily, Macafee banged the door on his way out of the room and Brian Tyson, roused, lifted his head.

Simultaneously the younger girl, the blonde they called Squeaky, lifted her eyes and sat up, scratching at her wildly disordered hair.

'What's happening?' she asked of Cameron Black who remained near the iron stove.

'It's all right,' Cam told her.

'It's just . . .' Squeaky said. She didn't have to say any more. Cameron Black knew what it just was: that at any minute the outpost could be overrun by dozens, hundreds of Comanche renegades. Sitting there, in her chemise, the striped Indian blanket pooled around her waist, she yawned, glanced at the other girl, Kate, and asked Cam, 'Is there any more coffee?'

'Some. It's not fresh, I'm afraid.'

'It doesn't matter. Where's Virginia?' she asked, looking around.

At that moment a woman's anguished cry rang out and was spent against the dawn sky. Mattie's baby had awakened and was making yet another effort to be born.

'Over there, with her,' Cameron said, turning his back as if that might help him to ignore matters.

There was a rustling of garments behind him and, after a moment, soft barefoot strides

44

approached. Squeaky tested the heat of the coffee pot with one finger, then poured herself a cup of the brew. Disheveled still, her blonde hair in disarray, she was an appealing girl, younger than Cameron had first guessed.

'I know that I look a mess,' Squeaky said, sipping from the coffee cup. 'I hate having only one dress, not having my hair brushes and pins. We had a lot of clothes with us . . . the Indians took them and burned the wagon.' She smiled dimly. 'I wonder what those Comanche women are wearing today! That would be a sight, wouldn't it?'

'I guess so,' Cam, lost in his own thoughts, responded. The girl nudged him with her elbow.

'Hey, what about the kid?' Squeaky asked. Brian, roused, sat with one elbow on the table, his chin cupped in his hand. 'Doesn't he get coffee?'

'He's Macafee's responsibility and none of mine,' Cameron said uncaringly. 'If you want to give him a cup, help yourself!'

Squeaky spared Cameron a critical glance, returned to the coffee pot and poured a cup for Brian Tyson. She returned to the table to sit beside the young prisoner. 'Come on, pal,' Cameron heard her say lightly. 'It might not turn out as bad as you think!'

45

In the next minute Lieutenant Young entered, looking even more haggard than the day before, not at all like the trim erect officer who had begun this tour of duty. He went directly to Cameron Black, declined an offer of coffee and spoke.

'Miss Scopes said that you wanted to talk to me.'

'I do,' Cameron said in a low voice. 'Let's sit over on that bench. Lieutenant, I think you have a problem.'

'A problem!' Young said, with a burst of harsh laughter. 'With the Comanches at the gate, no relief in sight, with only a bunch of untrustworthy deserters to man the outpost against the renegades, with my wife on the very brink of death – you think I might have a problem!'

Cameron took the young officer by the arm. 'This is something new and different. We need to talk about it.'

With a shrug, Lieutenant Young followed Cameron to the long bench against the far wall where formerly ladies had seated themselves waiting for young army officers to approach them to ask the pleasure of a dance. Young, Cameron Black decided, must have been one of these. The officer seated himself wearily, placing his cap beside him.

Cameron Black placed one boot on the bench, tilted his hat back and told him of his suspicions.

'It's my understanding,' he began, 'that these women, the "hostesses",' he said, groping for a words 'were in the habit of showing up here in their wagon when payday fell.'

Young nodded.

'I have also been told that the normal payday proceedings this time were disrupted because that was the very day that Colonel Hayes ordered the troop mounted because of the renegade trouble.'

'That is correct,' Young answered, rubbing at his eyes, 'although I don't understand—'

Cameron held up a hand, asking for patience. 'That's what I thought. So, Lieutenant, the payroll has not been distributed and therefore is secured somewhere within the outpost.'

'Also correct,' Young said, frowning with growing unease. 'I don't quite see what point you are trying to make.'

'Don't you?' Cameron looked around as the dark-haired girl, Kate, rose from her bed and began to dress. Squeaky and Brian Tyson still sat together at the table, speaking in low voices. He went on, 'Now this man Hazzard and the two other deserters have returned to the outpost. Why is that?'

47

'I suppose they couldn't get past the renegades,' Young said uneasily. He was beginning to get Cameron's drift.

'That could be a part of it,' Black agreed, lowering himself to sit beside the officer. 'But suppose that along the trail, they got to discussing matters and realized that only you and Demarest were holding the fort and that inside was the month's payroll, money they could put to good use. They knew that you were distracted by your wife's troubles, that Corporal Demarest is not well. If they could return before Colonel Hayes could reach the outpost, why, the payroll would be easy pickings.'

Cameron lowered his voice still more. 'Very early this morning I saw a man sneaking around the headquarters building. I didn't see him well enough to identify him and I could not say exactly what he was up to, but it was very suspicious to me. In what army do soldiers rise before they are summoned and lurk about?'

Young paled, his hands seemed to shake slightly.

'I'm not quite through,' Cameron Black said, although he wished he were. 'I have nothing to base this on ... but suppose Hazzard and the others did actually encounter some of the renegades? We know that one man did not return with them, so that is possible. What I have considered is this: what if they were able to come to an agreement with the Comanches? To let them pass with the stolen payroll in exchange for access to the weapons in the armory?'

'My God! That's treason,' Young said, defeat drawing his features down.

'Yes. I have no proof whatsoever, mind you. But just consider – what would be easier than for a band of renegades – the gates to the post let open to admit them – to swarm the armory and defeat the two isolated men left to guard it?'

'Yes,' Young said miserably, 'and I can see that the blame would fall entirely on the Comanches, not on Hazzard and the others.' His expression grew even more distraught. 'My wife and unborn child would be . . . Oh, Lord. It's not so important as these considerations, of course, but my career would be ended as well, wouldn't it? If I lived, it would be in disgrace while the deserters rode toward the Mexican border with the payroll, having left the blame on the Indians.'

There was no way to console the man, and Cameron did not even try. He only said, 'As I have told you – I have no proof. But you must be alert for any sign that they're up to dirty work.'

'Yes, yes, of course you're right.' Both men rose. Looking around the broad room, the young officer asked, 'If it comes to a fight, would the marshal be willing to stand with us. For that matter, would you?'

'That would make only four of us still,' Cameron reflected. He offered a half-smile to the lieutenant. 'Speaking for myself, however, I'll fight if it comes to it. There's no choice. I'm cornered here myself.'

And that he was. His horse was injured; there was a posse of men after him. If the posse didn't get him, then the renegades would. He had no place to go, and there was . . . his eyes lifted to the doorway as a night-weary Virginia Scopes entered, blinked into the shadows trying to adjust her vision following the harsh brightness of the desert dawn beyond, and crossed the room, holding a shawl tightly across her shoulders.

'One last word, Lieutenant,' Cameron said, 'if I am right, it will all happen quite soon. They can't risk Colonel Hayes' return.'

'No, no, you're right.' Young ran his fingers through his dark hair. 'Will you talk to Marshal Macafee for me? Tell him what you suspect?'

'I think it would be better if you did it yourself,'

Black told him. He did not believe that Macafee truly trusted him. Why would he? They had tangled once before, long ago in Taos. Originally Cameron had meant to flee the outpost before something jogged the lawman's memory concerning the encounter, but now it was impossible.

Everything was quite impossible, he thought, as he strode across the ballroom to where Virginia stood watching his approach with uncertain eyes.

Everything.

FOUR

'Can't you do something for this man!' Squeaky asked, as Cameron neared the stove. The blonde girl indicated the weary Brian Tyson. 'He's been manacled to this table leg for a day and a night.'

Cameron shook his head. 'It's not up to me. I'll go up to the parapet and relieve the marshal on lookout, but I doubt he'll be inclined to just let him loose.'

Virginia had poured the dregs of the coffee pot into a cup and stood scowling at Cameron, at Squeaky, at the universe.

'How's the lieutenant's woman?' Cameron asked.

'No change. I think we're going to have to do something soon. To bring the baby out, that is.

Cam . . . you've delivered calves, haven't you? Out on the range?'

'Hold on!' Cameron Black said. 'That's hardly the same thing.'

'It's more than I've ever done,' Virginia said. 'How long can that girl be expected to endure this! She'll die, Cameron,' she added in a low voice, the tin cup in her hand shaking so that she had to bring her free hand up to keep it from spilling down the front of her dress.

'I don't know anything about it,' Cameron said in a muffled voice, keeping his eyes to the floor. 'I once saw a Navajo woman deliver, but that was a normal birth. This one, with the baby backwards, I wouldn't even think about trying it.'

'If it offered the mother – and child – even a small chance at making it, Cameron?' Virginia asked. 'Who else is there here to even attempt it?'

'If it came down to that . . .' Cameron said, shaking his head heavily, not ready to accept that kind of burden, but unable to decline. 'If there's ever the point where you think those are the only options, yes,' he said, cursing himself silently, 'I would try it, given Young's authorization.'

And if he were to fail, Lieutenant Young would damn him forever. The front door to the ballroom stood open and Black, shifting his eyes that way to avoid looking at Virginia Scopes, saw two shadowy figures walking slowly away from the building, their heels kicking up tiny puffs of pale dust. The sky was growing white, but there was still a blur of color low on the dawn horizon.

'You'd better talk to her,' Cameron Black said.

'What do you mean?' Virginia asked. She glanced first at Squeaky who continued to sit next to the young prisoner, speaking in a low voice. Then she saw that Cameron was watching through the door as Kate crossed the parade ground, arm in arm with the pale-haired deserter, Harding. 'She's paid to talk to men. What's so different about this?'

'I can't tell you right now,' Cameron answered, 'but you better have a talk with her. Tell her to cool her heels for a while. I think she's getting ready to ride off with the man.'

'What is it you know that you're not telling me?' Virginia demanded, grabbing his ann.

'It's what I don't know,' Cameron said. 'It's all guesswork, but you'd better have a talk with that young lady, advise her to remain here.'

'Where it's safe!' Virginia laughed recklessly.

'Talk to her. I agreed to your proposition, much

as it scares me. Do me this favor in return. That girl's getting herself into more trouble than she could possibly know.'

Virginia nodded solemnly, then looked again at Squeaky and Brian Tyson, wondering how much trouble her other girl might be getting herself into. 'I'll try,' Virginia promised Cameron Black. 'But it's kind of hard to warn someone when you don't know what you're warning them against.'

'Just tell her to stay put,' Cameron growled in a voice more rough than he intended. Then he went out into the bright morning sunlight himself and started across the parade ground toward the stable. The gray horse eyed him miserably as he entered, made a quick inspection of the animal's wounded rump, forked some fresh hay down for it and went out again, this time carrying his spanking new Winchester '73 rifle. He had no liking for those army-issue Springfields. It had always puzzled him as to why when newer, far superior weapons were available, the army continued to give their soldiers the outdated breech-loaders. It must have had something to do with politics, maybe there was a stockpile of the .45–70s somewhere that someone had decided must be issued rather than leaving them in the warehouse.

Only trouble was, these days the Indians were more likely to he carrying the new repeaters than the soldiers. Cameron walked heavily toward the parapet. The sun was already warm on his back in this desert country. He was aware of his stomach's rumbling. When had he last eaten?

Lieutenant Young had once again gone back to sit beside his wife. You couldn't really blame the young officer, but it was a hell of a way to command an army outpost. From the corner of his eye, Cameron saw Virginia and Kate in close conversation, standing in the ribbon of shade cast by the awning in front of the old sutler's store.

And where were the three deserters at that moment: Harding, Jason and Hazzard? Plotting their next move? Cameron Black liked none of this.

Marshal Macafee, glowering, stood waiting for Cameron as he ascended the ladder to the parapet. 'Who's watching the kid?'

'You,' Cameron said. 'I thought we should switch jobs.'

A little of the heat went out of Macafee's voice. 'It's a hell of a thing, isn't it?' he asked. 'Lieutenant Young told me what you suspect,' he clarified. 'If Hazzard and his boys do what you think they have in mind and slip out, leaving the gates open, well . . . we'll all be massacred, won't we? And none of it will matter anymore.' The marshal shook his head, and his eyes met Cameron's. 'I mean, the kid who'll they surely hang for trying to do the right thing, for what he thought his boss had ordered him to do, if I take him in.

'Or . . .' he added, 'whatever might become of Cameron Black.'

'Figured it out finally, did you?'

'I knew you right off Black. Just couldn't give you a name or remember exactly where we had met before. Now I've got it.'

'Taos was a long time ago,' was all that Cameron could think to say.

'The law might not think that matters.'

'They might not.' Cameron grinned crookedly, 'But you aren't going to take two prisoners across the desert, not when I'm one of them.'

'Maybe not,' the marshal agreed, stroking his long silver mustache with thumb and forefinger. 'Maybe not. I suppose you might be more of a handful than that kid down there. It's been interesting talking to you, Black. We'll have to have a longer conversation when there's more time.'

*

Beside the old sutler's store Virginia Scopes had finally cornered Kate, and she grabbed the younger woman by the arm, turning her to face her. Virginia had not taken the time to pin her hair up and the dry desert wind drifted it across her face as she pressed Kate back against the wall of the old store.

'What do you want!' Kate demanded. 'Why don't you leave me alone?'

'Are you planning on running away? Tell me?'

'Who told you that?' Kate asked, but her eyes did not meet Virginia's.

'It's rumored.'

'It was Squeaky, wasn't it? The little snitch!'

'Never mind who it was. Answer me, you ungrateful wretch!'

'Ungrateful!' Kate scoffed. 'Why, because you picked me up off the street and dressed me in silk and sent me to work? Oh, yes, Virginia, I thank you – for ruining my life.'

'You would have starved on your own,' Virginia replied. 'Answer my question, Kate. Are you planning on running away?'

'Yes!' the dark-haired girl answered explosively. 'If that's what you want to call it. I'm planning on leaving you. Is that running away? Do you think I want to end up like you in another ten years? I have a chance now, Virginia, to get free.' Briefly her eyes softened and she searched Virginia Scopes' eyes for understanding.

'I met Aaron Harding out here last month. He cares for me, Virginia – not like these other men. He wants me to go away with him, and I told him that I would.'

Virginia sighed and let her hands fall away from the dark-eyed woman in red. 'Where will you go, Kate? How will you survive? There are hostile Indians out there, and Harding would be only an army deserter on the run.'

'He knows what he's doing,' Kate said, her anger returning. 'He told me he knows a way through the Comanche lines, and I believe him. He has money. We are going to purchase some land and build a house on it. Have a normal life! Can't you see how much I want that, Virginia? Haven't you ever longed for such a simple thing?'

Virginia nodded but did not answer. Everything that Cameron had suspected then seemed to be true. And Kate, desperate enough to take the chance, was going to ride with the deserters. She tried once more.

'You'll be riding with an outlaw, Kate. Can't you

see that? There can be no such thing as a normal life when you're on the run. The army will track him down sooner or later and you'll be left with nothing.'

'I have nothing now,' Kate said, tearing herself away from Virginia Scopes. 'Nothing at all.'

Then she stalked away and Virginia could only watch her go. Hell, she thought angrily, maybe the little fool is right! Maybe she, herself, should once have ridden away with her outlaw lover. Shaking that long-ago regret from her mind, she started back toward Mattie Young's quarters.

Squeaky sat nearly head to head with Brian Tyson, her hand on his. 'My friend Kate wants me to try to escape with her,' Squeaky told him quietly, looking around to see if anyone was listening. 'She says that at least we have a chance that way. That we have none here in the outpost once the renegades decide to attack.'

'Go then,' Brian Tyson said without looking at the blonde girl. His voice was low, uninflected. 'Why should I care what you do?'

'I don't know.' She hesitated. 'I just thought that you might.'

'I don't!' Brian said loudly enough so that he

could be heard across the room. His free hand folded itself into a tight fist. 'You're talking to a dead man, Squeaky. If you've a chance to save yourself, take it.'

'Maybe I will!' she said, with some heat. She started to rise but lowered herself again onto the bench and reached for his fisted hand, petting it gently until the fist relaxed itself and she took his fingers in her own.

The relative silence was broken by a loud cry from the rampart beyond the open door of the ballroom.

'Riders coming in!'

Both Marshal Macafee and Corporal Demarest, who had been half asleep on one of the long benches, lurched to their feet, grabbed their weapons and charged the door. Above, they saw Cameron Black crouched, his rifle leveled through a gap in the pointed palisade logs. They scrambled that way as Lieutenant Young, hatless, rushed across the parade ground to join them.

Cameron watched the others arrive from the corner of his eyes as he leveled his sights. Two men, riding hell for it, whipped their ponies toward the outpost. Behind them, breaking from the trees, was a party of five renegade Comanches.

61

Only two of these were mounted, and one of the horses even at this distance was identifiable as a US Army bay, perhaps the one that had belonged to the missing deserter.

The incoming riders looked hopefully toward the outpost. The man in the lead was sitting a badly faltering roan. The one behind, a slower dun. They would be lucky if they even made the fort.

Lieutenant Young yelled to Demarest, 'Get down there, ready to swing a gate open.' Then he worked his way toward Cameron Black, wanting to ask a question, but Cameron had no time for conversation.

The front bead sight of his Winchester settled into the V on the rear sight and he tracked the first renegade rider. He touched off and the .44-40 bullet struck the Indian in the chest and he fell from the saddle of the bay, arms flung wide. Beside Cameron, Lieutenant Young's .45–70 fired, and one of the running Comanches buckled up, holding his leg.

'Open the gates!' Young shouted down to Demarest as he frantically fumbled another load into the breech of his Springfield rifle.

Cameron Black levered three more rounds

through his Winchester, but the Indians had turned away and were racing back toward the shelter of the trees, and he doubted that he had hit anything with those shots.

The inriders had achieved the gate and now it was closed and barred behind them as the weary horseman swung to the ground. Before Cameron had even reached the bottom rung 36 of the ladder he recognized them and his jaw muscles clenched. Lieutenant Young was greeting them. Marshal Macafee was nearly on Cameron's heels as he strode slowly toward the new arrivals.

One of these was a broad-faced man with pale eyes wearing a leather coat and faded black jeans. He was wiping at his sweating face and throat with a red kerchief. His companion was a younger, wiry man in a dirty blue shirt, blue trousers. The younger man nudged the other as Cameron approached.

'Well, I'll he damned! Just who we were looking for,' he said, and he drew his revolver, grinning at Cameron without humor.

'Hello, Lacey,' Black said. The lieutenant and Marshal Macafee exchanged questioning glances. Black nodded again. 'How are you, Douglas. Close call, was it?'

'The hell with all that,' the man named Lacey said. He took two strides toward Cameron and said: 'Unbelt your guns, Black.'

Cameron asked quietly, 'Why would I want to do that, Lacey?'

'Because if you don't, I'll shoot you where you stand,' Lacey responded. Cameron Black shook his head and smiled.

'Yes, but as long as I have my Colts, I'll have a chance to fire back after I'm hit. You won't get me to disarm, Lacey. If you want to go to shooting, have at it,' Black said, and the smile was gone from his face. He was braced and ready.

'What is all of this?' Lieutenant Young demanded. 'I won't have any of this nonsense here.'

'This man's a killer, Lieutenant. Cameron Black is his name if he never gave it to you. We are what's left of a posse which has been tracking him since Victorville where he gunned down an innocent man.'

'He was a rustler,' Cameron said softly.

'So Boss Norman claimed!' Lacey said heatedly. 'The kid was only a dumb sodbuster looking for a milk cow for his family.'

'And so he decided to rustle one of Norman's

64

cows,' Black said. His attention had not wavered from Lacey's pistol. If he eared back the hammer on his Colt, Black knew he would have to move, draw and fire at once.

'Norman owns half of Hidalgo County. He could afford to lose one cow! The kid needed one for his wife and kids.'

'Then he should have bought one,' Black answered evenly. His words belied his own convictions. Norman had gone overboard, but then the range boss had wanted to send a message to other would-be rustlers in the area – they would not be allowed to get away with taking his beeves.

Lacey seemed suddenly aware of the white-mustached man standing behind and to the side of Cameron Black. Sunlight glinted on Macafee's silver marshal's badge.

'You, you're bound to uphold the law; help us take this man in.'

Macafee just stared coldly at Lacey. 'Victorville is way out of my jurisdiction. I'd have to see some legal papers.'

On the plankwalk in front of the ballroom, Kate and Squeaky, still in their faded finery, stood watching, the wind shifting their bright-colored skirts. Lacey tried again.

'Lieutenant? Surely the army can help us here? Place this man in the stockade until we can gather the legal documents we need. Post men to watch him at least, so he doesn't escape.'

'I don't see this as a military matter in any sense,' Lieutenant Young said. 'As for guarding him ... we haven't anyone at all available to do that.'

'What about them?' Lacey said, growing more exasperated. Eyes turned toward the barracks where Hazzard, Jason and Aaron Harding sat slouched on a bench, watching the proceedings.

'If I had men to watch a stockade, those three would be in it at this moment,' Young said.

Lacey smothered a curse. Macafee tried to explain things. 'Lacey, we are very short on men. Those you see here are all we have to protect this fort. I don't think it would be doing anyone a service to disarm or incarcerate Cameron Black just now. Do you? He saved you boys out there just now, and if the Indians come again, you'll be happy to have him at your side in the fight.'

'I'd just as soon ...' Lacey snarled. Then, angrily, he holstered his pistol and asked Young, 'You don't mind if we stable our horses, do you, Lieutenant?' Nodding to his co-rider he said bitterly, 'Come on, Douglas. Let's find the stable. It's got to smell better in there.'

The two gathered the reins to their tired horses and started walking toward the back of the fort. There was a loud, jeering laugh from the barracks. Hazzard waved a derogatory hat at the posse men.

'There's someone I'd like to shoot,' Macafee said with uncharacteristic savageness, his eyes fixed on Hazzard. 'At least these bounty riders believe they're doing the right thing.' Cameron thought he heard the lawman mutter 'pig' again, his epithet for the deserters. Then he spun on his heel and stalked back toward the ballroom.

'That was a near thing,' Young said to Cameron. 'Is anything they said true, or. . . ?'

Virginia Scopes appeared in front of the base officers' quarters, frantically waving a towel.

'Cameron!' she shouted. 'You have to come here now. Mattie's taken a turn for the worse!'

FIVE

The young woman no longer screamed in pain. She was inert, dishrag-limp on the perspiration-soaked sheet. Lieutenant Young was beside himself, waxen and frantic with concern. Virginia, on her knees beside the bed, looked up at them and said, 'Something has to be done, and now, Cameron. She's beginning to bleed heavily.'

'Young?' Black asked.

'I don't . . . I can't. Can you help, Black?'

'I can try,' Cameron was all he could say to the young officer. 'I'm not ready, hardly willing and I'm not sure if I'm able. That's not much of a comfort, but I just don't know. I'll try, if you say so.'

'Lieutenant!' Virginia said, her eyes pleading. 'You have to let him try. She can't last much longer this way.'

Long minutes passed as Young studied his wife's pallid face, saw the slow stain of blood seeping onto the sheets. Black could read his thoughts. To leave his wife in the hands of a stranger from the desert, one with no medical training at all was tantamount to killing Mattie himself.

There was no choice. Without speaking he nodded assent to Black.

Virginia was to her feet now, and she asked, 'What do you need, Cam?'

'Hot water, soap, plenty of towels. Pair of scissors, twine of some sort. Better make it fast, Ginnie,' he said, slipping into the old-time use of her nickname. She nodded and hurried to the BOQ pantry to look for the items.

A haggard Young asked, 'What can I do?'

'Just get out of here,' Cameron Black said as he unbuckled his twin Colts and rolled up his sleeves. 'See to your fort.'

'If anything goes wrong. . . .' he began. It was half a hope, half a threat.

'Yeah, I know,' Cameron said, as Virginia searched the cupboards in the background, 'now, do as I told you, get out of here. You'd be less than no help.'

Young paused, kissed his tormented wife's forehead and then stalked out into the bright sunlight, closing the door gently behind him.

'The water will take a few minutes to heat, Cam,' Virginia said on her return. She laid the other items he had requested on the bedside table. She looked up at him nervously and asked, 'What are you going to do?'

'*Try* to do,' he corrected. 'If it were a calving gone wrong, I'd turn the unborn critter around. That's the only way to do it.' He added grimly, 'This little girl is a lot smaller than a cow.'

There was concern on his sun-tanned, weather-lined face, and in his eyes. Virginia touched his shoulder briefly, reassuringly.

'The water's boiling,' she said, and her hand fell away. Cameron Black rolled his sleeves up even further and whispered the only prayer he knew, following it with a muffled curse.

'We can't wait any longer,' the deserter, Jason, said to Hazzard. The balding soldier paced the ground as Hazzard and Aaron Harding watched from the bench in front of the barracks. 'When we planned this there was only the two of them – Young and Corporal Demarest. Now look! The marshal, this gunfighter, whoever he is, and these two new men.' Concern was etched in Jason's beefy face. He stopped his pacing and halted in front of Hazzard, his arms akimbo. 'Well?'

'You're right, Jason. We'll do it tonight.' The broad-shouldered Hazzard stretched his arms and turned toward Harding. 'What did you tell that little squiff?'

'Don't call her that!' He muted his voice. 'I didn't tell Kate nothing.'

'What are you going to do about her?' Hazzard demanded.

'Do?' Harding seemed baffled. 'I'm taking her with me.'

'Last thing we need's a woman along!' Jason said angrily. Hazzard nodded in silent agreement.

'No woman.'

'To hell with both of you,' Harding said, rising from his lounging position. The blond kid was trembling. 'She goes with me. We get past the renegades, we split the dough. You two go where you want, I'll go where I want, do what I want – and Kate goes with me.'

The young man stalked away then, toward the front door of the barracks.

'It's trouble,' Jason muttered. 'Can you imagine a grown man hypnotized like that by a skirt?'

'It happens,' Hazzard said lazily. Then he also rose and clapped a hand on Jason's shoulder. 'Don't worry about it. She won't be going with us. I'll see to that.'

When John Macafee returned to the ballroom he saw his prisoner still sitting side by side with the girl they called Squeaky. He supposed that he should have broken it up, but what was the harm? He doubted that they were plotting an escape. If not for the forlorn set of Brian Tyson's face, you might have thought they were only two schoolkids in the throes of first love.

Macafee had barely seated himself on one of the benches, his hat placed to the side when the two newcomers, Lacey and Douglas, stormed into the room.

'Any coffee?' Lacey demanded of Macafee, as if he were an employee.

'Not unless you brought some,' Macafee answered, swallowing his distaste for the big-shouldered bounty man.

'So happens we did,' Lacey replied, throwing down the saddle-bags he had been carrying over his shoulder. 'You'd think the army would have coffee, wouldn't you?'

Macafee didn't answer as Lacey unbuckled his saddle-bag and withdrew a cheesecloth packet. He tossed this to Douglas. 'Boil us up some coffee,' he ordered the uncertain youth.

Douglas seemed bewildered. Weeks on the desert pursuing the elusive Cameron Black, followed by a skirmish with the renegades which had left two of their party dead, seemed to have taken the heart out of him. He glanced wistfully at Squeaky who sat even more closely to Brian Tyson now, holding his arm with both of her hands.

'Who's that?' Lacey asked, sitting uninvited and unwelcome beside Marshal Macafee.

'Prisoner,' Macafee answered.

'Treat your prisoners pretty well, don't you?' Lacey said, loud enough for everyone to hear. 'They all get pretty little blondes, do they?'

'Shut up,' Macafee muttered, crossing his arms and closing his eyes. He felt the bench rock as Lacey got up and walked over to the stove where Douglas was trying to prod the fire to life.

He heard Lacey say, 'The marshal can take a kid like that down, but when it comes to a gunman like Cameron Black, he just pretty much ignores him.'

Macafee's eyes flickered open and he said coldly, 'I guess you didn't hear me when I asked you to shut up. I can't stand a man who shoots off his mouth when he don't know what he's talking about.'

He had barely closed his eyes again when he heard the rustling of fabric and he lifted his gaze to see Squeaky standing over him. She slid beside him on the bench and asked in a low, nervous voice: 'Can't you unshackle him for awhile? He's been chained up there for almost thirty hours.' Macafee shook his head negatively. 'But why?' Squeaky demanded. 'Look, Marshal, he's just a kid. He wouldn't make any trouble for anyone.'

'He already did,' Macafee answered. 'He killed a man in cold blood.'

'He told me all about it,' Squeaky said, persisting. 'What would you have done in his situation?'

'Maybe called the man out, given him a chance,' Macafee answered.

'But you're an experienced man! Brian isn't. He saw a woman being attacked, and his boss had warned him to watch over her. I wouldn't exactly call it cold blood. He was nervous, scared for the girl.'

'Maybe some on the jury will see it that way,' Macafee said. 'Me – I can't let him loose. He might decide to grab another gun and decide he's justified in killing me as well. That isn't the way the law works, girl. Go back and hold his hand – that's all you can do for him.'

A tiny hiss escaped from between Squeaky's teeth as she rose again and swept away. Macafee again tried dozing off. He was confident in the way he was conducting his duty, but vaguely uneasy as well. But then, he reflected, no one had appointed him judge and jury. He did his job. That was it.

The sky was already darkening when Cameron Black emerged from the BOQ, still without his guns. Lieutenant Young who had been watching the sky, moving from point to point around the outpost, his nerves shattered, watched Black deliberately roll his sleeves down and lean against the wall. Black looked defeated, angry and frustrated at once. Young tried to hold back, but he could take no more. He took three strides across the shadowed parade ground and heard the struggling cry of a baby. Thin and high, astonished at this new world it had entered, the cry rose in volume as if demanding an explanation of events. Lieutenant Young broke briefly into a run and then slowed himself, regaining his military composure. He walked directly to Black who lifted haggard eyes at his approach.

'It's a boy,' Black said in a weary voice.

'How is—'

'I don't know, Young. It was a rough bit of work. I think Mattie will be all right – but it will take some time.'

Young scowled, 'But you're not sure?'

'No,' Black admitted, 'I'm not sure.'

Young nodded heavily, looked uncertainly at the closed door and said, 'I'd like to go in – to see them.'

'It should be all right. Virginia probably has them mostly cleaned up.'

'Cleaned up?' Young asked dimly.

Black nodded. There was no point at that moment in telling the young officer how much blood Mattie had lost, how slim the chances of her making it through this ordeal were. The child at least looked healthy, though how anyone was to nurse it was a mystery. He grabbed Young's arm and said with utmost weariness, 'I did my best, Young.'

The officer rushed into the room and Black followed heavily. He knew that the arrival of a tiny red, wrinkled stranger was never enough to compensate for the loss of a beloved wife.

76

Sometimes this could even turn to resentment against the baby. Or against the attending physician.

Virginia had indeed done a good job of cleaning up. Mattie lay still and apparently at peace beneath clean white sheets, her hair brushed. Her eyes did not flicker open, nor did she respond when Young took her hand. Beside the bed Virginia sat holding the tiny, squalling infant which turned its head frantically looking for nourishment and the comfort of its mother's breast. Virginia glanced at Black who shrugged with his eyes. Young seemed shattered, defeated. There was an unhealthy pallor about Mattie and her breath was very shallow. Neither Black nor Virginia could think of anything to say that might comfort the young officer. The room remained as silent as a chapel; beyond the doorway, the rising desert wind whispered a dirge.

The first shot roused them all to action.

Cameron lunged for his gunbelt, buckled it on and snatched up his Winchester.

Young, deep in his own misery a moment before, was galvanized into action. They reached the door in time to see the gates swung open and the escaping men whipping their horses toward the open flats beyond. By the purple light of dusk, they saw two figures collapsed on the parade ground. Aaron Harding lay sprawled in the dust. Kate was kneeling over him, her folded hands uplifted, sobs racking her body. The door to the headquarters building stood open and Black had no doubt that the safe had been cracked, that Hazzard had taken the payroll. There was no sign of a guard on the ramparts. It seemed certain that Demarest had been killed as well.

Several men had appeared on the plankwalk in front of the ballroom: Marshal Macafee, Lacey and Douglas. Young treated them as if they were conscripts.

'Get the gates closed and man the ramparts!' he shouted frantically. 'Unless I miss my guess, the Comanches will make their attack now!'

Cameron Black listened, watched, and then touched Young's shoulder lightly.

'What is it?' Young asked with deep irritation.

'Have the men ready to open the gates again for me in a few minutes. I'll be riding out.'

'Riding out? Are you crazy! What do you mean, Black? You're not deserting me, too?'

'No, sir. I figure the colonel would like to find that the payroll has been recovered, that the army can't blame you for losing that or the fort. I'm riding after Hazzard, sir, and I will find him.'

Squeaky had rushed out of the ballroom on the heels of the men and now she ran barefoot across the parade ground to sink down beside Kate who alternately stroked Aaron Harding's forehead and prayed frantically to her God. The praying would do no good now; Harding was obviously quite dead, open eyes fixed on the darkening desert sky, his body growing cold.

'What happened, Kate?' Squeaky demanded of her friend. 'What went wrong?'

'He was really going to take me away from everything,' Kate said, bowing her head. 'He told me. I believed him if no one else did. We were going to start a new life together.'

'What happened?' Squeaky asked again. She was now kneeling beside her friend as night settled and the men scurried about.

'Aaron came to me and told me to be ready, that Hazzard was going to pop the safe holding the payroll. It was the right time – Lieutenant Young was so distressed by his wife's labor that he was paying no attention to anything going on around him. The only other man they had to fear – Cameron Black – was trying to play midwife to Mattie Young. There was only the man on guard,

Corporal Demarest, to worry about.

'Jason said that he could take care of the old trooper, and I guess he did, because no cry was raised from the parapet as Hazzard crossed to the headquarters building, jimmied the door and slipped inside to get at the safe. Aaron stood guard outside. I stood near to him, trembling, but he told me that it would be all right. In less than an hour we would be free.

'Well, it took that long at least for Hazzard to open the safe, but when he emerged he had two saddle-bags. He tossed one of these to Aaron and we started for the horses. "One minute", Hazzard said as we started to mount, "I told you that the woman isn't going. She'll slow us down".

'Aaron said, "She damn well is going. We'll split up as soon as we clear the outpost. She won't be any trouble to you".

'There was some more arguing,' Kate told Squeaky, 'and I was about ready to give it up so that Aaron wouldn't scuffle with them, but it had gone on too long. Maybe they just wanted to have a bigger split of the money for themselves; maybe it was all about me!' She paused, gulping in deep breaths of air. 'But whatever it was, both of them – Jason and Hazzard – drew their pistols while Aaron

80

was tightening the cinches to my horse. One of them triggered off and shot him in the back. He ran; I ran after him. He died where you see him. Hazzard and Jason rode off.'

Squeaky looked down at the still form of the young Aaron Harding, shook her head and rose, dusting off her skirts. Kate grabbed her hand. Her eyes were moist, her voice shaky.

'Squeaky, don't let them take your young man away from you. Do whatever it takes, but don't let them take him.' Then she bowed her head, buried her face in her hands and began sobbing again. Squeaky walked away toward the ballroom. No one would be watching Brian Tyson now. Every man was standing watch for the renegades. She glanced around, seeing activity along the parapet but nowhere else. Lifting her skirts higher she hurried on more determined than ever.

Cameron Black returned to the stable and saddled his gray horse. The animal seemed still resentful, but also eager to be moving. The arrow wound it had suffered was healing nicely, Cameron noted. He was grim as he led the horse from the shelter, weary from the hours of unaccustomed work of trying to deliver Mattie's baby – a tedious, cautious sort of task to which he was not suited. This, he thought, was more his speed – tracking down the deserters.

It was not the payroll that he considered, but the appeal for help in Kate's eyes. Those two young people, such as they were, had deserved better than having Harding shot down cruelly. In a distant way Cameron also found himself concerned with Lieutenant Young's position. The young officer had done his best under the circumstances, with what he had to work with. His career would likely be over once it was discovered that he had let the deserters take the payroll because he had been too distracted by his wife's troubles. The army was not known for sentiment.

There was a moment as he led his horse across the parade ground that Cameron considered his own position, considered that he might be better riding free, away from the fort. After all, there were still the bounty hunters to consider – they called themselves a posse, but he knew them for what they were. A price had been placed on his head, and these two and their dead partners had no thought of avenging the death of a naive sodbuster, but only in making a few dollars which they figured for an easy play, the four of them against a lone rider. Cameron had no doubt that they would be willing to shoot him from behind and claim whatever price the law in Victorville had put on his head.

Why would he return with the payroll, if that were possible? How much did he care about Young? If Mattie didn't pull through, the lieutenant, far from thanking him, would despise him for his failed effort. The bounty hunters would be waiting for him. Why would he return? The desert was dark, wide and open. There were a handful of renegades still prowling, but they could not catch his big gray horse, and he knew it.

He caught a glimpse of Virginia Scopes standing in front of Mattie's room, her arms crossed beneath her breasts. Their eyes met only briefly, and then both turned their glances aside.

Why would he return?

SIX

Lieutenant Young, Marshal Macafee, Lacey and Douglas stood in a loose group watching Cameron Black as he swung into leather and walked the big gray horse toward the gates.

'What's he doing?' Lacey demanded. 'Lieutenant, you can't let him ride out! He's a wanted man.'

'I have no authority to stop him,' Young said. 'Even if I wished to.' He himself walked to the gates to drop the bar and allow Black to pass through.

'Marshal?' Lacey tried frantically.

'It's none of my business,' Macafee said drily.

'Then, by God, we're going after him.'

'Then you'd better have fast horses saddled and ready to run,' Macafee advised him. 'He'll be gone in minutes. I saw the shape your ponies were in when you rode in. Let it go, Lacey. There's nothing you can do, and I don't really think you want to go riding out there on this night.'

For again they heard the yipping of the renegade Comanches imitating coyotes as they passed their messages. It seemed to Macafee that there were now more of them out there prowling. To the returning officer he said, 'Lieutenant, I think we ought to he getting up onto the ramparts.'

Whatever deal Hazzard had made, or thought he had made with the renegades, made no difference. The poorly armed, desperate Comanches had no choice but to storm the outpost and try to take its armory if they were to have a chance against Colonel Hayes and his company of men.

Young was aware of the added burden he bore. To let the armory fall would be doubly censorious. The payroll could be replaced; to let those rifles slip into the hands of the renegades enabling them to conduct efficient raids and warfare would be completely inexcusable. His career would be effectively ended even if he did not face criminal charges.

No man could have felt as low as Young did as he climbed the ladder to the parapet. Across the desert night as the signal calls of the renegades fell to silence, one voice continued. A newborn baby cried for nurture, for its mother, and Young did not even know if the struggling infant would have a living mother come sunrise.

Cameron Black hunched his shoulders against the chill of night. Many newcomers were surprised at the rapidity with which temperatures could alter in the light atmosphere of the desert. It was not uncommon for daytime temperatures of 110 degrees and plus to drop to freezing overnight. He was not unprepared. His buffalo coat was now on his shoulders, and if not warm, he was comfortable.

Even by starlight he was able to follow the deep tracks Hazzard and Jason's horses had cut in the red sand. These, quite obviously were not tending toward the woods where the renegades hid, but veered drastically northward, in the direction of Santa Fe. Either there had been no bargain between the deserters and the Comanches, or Hazzard had chosen deliberately to break it: the latter seemed more likely.

Hazzard and Jason would be trusting to their horses to easily outdistance the renegades, who, according to all that Cameron Black had observed, possessed only a few stolen horses. Comanches prefered to fight on horseback, compared to their brothers, the Apaches, whose desert world made fighting afoot preferable, but these renegades – probably mostly young untested braves who had broken out from the reservation to protest conditions, or to seek the same glory in battle that their fathers spoke of, were ill-equipped, ill-mounted, and poorly armed. All reasons for them to strike the fort. If they had known how undermanned it was, the stockade would certainly have fallen days earlier, even to these few raiders. It seemed to Black that they must have been holding out a hope that some other warriors, perhaps those of the larger party now being pursued by Colonel Hayes, would arrive to reinforce them before they made their assault. By now they must have realized that they could expect no help, and they would have to make the decision to attack soon or withdraw in disgrace.

All of these thoughts ran through Black's mind as he methodically trailed the two deserters across dry arroyos, sand-swept knolls and rocky washes.

The renegades would not care about his scalp, but the big gray horse would offer a great inducement – it, and the guns he carried.

His long gun, the Winchester, rode in its saddle scabbard. In the dark of night he was unlikely to be offered the opportunity for a shot at any great distance, less likely to hit his target. His belt guns, on the other hand, were ready for instant use. The skirts of his heavy coat were swept back, leaving both holsters accessible. For a moment Black rued the damage done to his left arm. For Virginia had been correct – he could no longer draw and fire with that hand. He had made a serious mistake in that gunfight down in Alamogordo and had paid for it. Habitually he held his reins in his right hand, his gun hand, and this would make him just a fraction of a second slower in going to leather if the occasion should arise.

The gray horse plodded on willingly, but it, too, was half a step slower, a little more uncertain than before it had been wounded. Two warriors, they were, gradually breaking down from the trials of their battles.

Lacey had been reconsidering their situation. Now he drew the increasingly uncertain Douglas aside as the two stood outside the shadowed ballroom.

'We're fools to stay here,' he said to the younger

man, gripping his arm tightly in his meaty hand. He glanced up to where Young and Marshal Macafee stood uneasy watch.

'We'd be fools to go out, the way they tell it,' Douglas objected nervously. Lacey scoffed at the idea.

'What? The Indians? Far as we've seen, far as anyone knows there's still no more than half a dozen, maybe ten renegades out there. We know they've got no ponies – outside of one old army horse. In the night, why would they rise up to follow us? They'll be happy to see more men deserting the outpost.'

'Maybe,' Douglas said. 'Maybe they'll jump us as soon as we clear the fort.' Douglas knew that he had gotten in over his head. At first joining the posse to chase down the gunman, Black, had seemed like an easy and respectable way to make some extra money to support his water-poor ranch. A few weeks on the desert had changed his mind. Now they were only two and there was no way to get back home.

'What's the point of it, anyway, Lacey?' the kid asked.

'Think about it!' Lacey hissed, tightening his grip on the younger man's shoulder so that he winced and tried to pull away. 'What'd we start out on this miserable trek for?'

'To nab Cameron Black,' Douglas said, twisting away and rubbing his arm.

'No. Why did we want to catch him? For the money, isn't that so?'

'I suppose so,' Douglas said dully. His arms hurt; the night was cold.

'You're not paying attention,' Lacey said with disgust. 'Where's Black now? Out chasing down a couple of deserters who stole the army payroll. Aren't you listening, Douglas? If Black runs them down, he'll be holding a small fortune.'

'Suppose they kill him?' Douglas asked doubtfully.

'Suppose they do? Then we have our chance. They'll have no way of knowing that we're on their trail too.'

'If we found them, shot them—'

'They're thieves. The army would give us a medal.'

'And Black?'

'There's a bounty on his head anyway, isn't there?'

'The payroll?' Douglas asked, growing interested.

'Who would know what happened to it? We blame Black. He won't be coming back to argue the point. Why, he's a wanted man anyway. It'll save the county the expense of a trial if he's killed out on the desert trying to steal an army payroll.' Lacey, his eyes shifting from Douglas to the ramparts where the watchers stood, asked, 'What do you say?'

'I say, we'd better get our ponies saddled before Cameron Black is clean out of the territory.'

When Squeaky re-entered the ballroom, only Brian Tyson was there. Shackled to the table leg still, his eyes reflected defeat. She rushed to his side. Her voice was a panting whisper.

'Brian, we have to get out of here.'

'How?' he asked lethargically.

'The way you got loose before,' she said, speaking rapidly. 'I'll lift the table leg and we can slip the shackle from underneath it. The marshal is busy watching for the Indians.'

'Squeaky,' Brian said wearily, 'what are we to do after that? Where are we to go?' Tyson shook his head. There was no way to escape, nowhere on the desert where they could find sanctuary. 'We have no horses, no hope of getting past the guarded gates.'

91

'We could try . . . something,' she said settling beside him again. 'We have to come up with a plan.' Her young eyes were eager, bright with dreams.

'You don't even know me,' Brian said.

'I'll bet I know you better than people who have known you all of your life. All the conversation we've had—'

'You don't even know me. I'm a killer, of no use to you, Squeaky. Find another man, one who can offer you a real chance at life.'

'Listen,' she said, scooting even closer to him, 'you made a mistake. You only did what you thought was right at the time.'

'That doesn't change anything – I'm still a murderer. Why would you waste your time even talking to me?'

'I don't know,' Squeaky said wearily. 'That's the way some girls are.'

Her eyes grew strangely bright and she pursed her lips. Then, without another word she bent forward so that her shoulder was under the table and she strained, lifting the heavy plank monstrosity upward until she could slip the iron shackle free once again. She straightened up, rubbing her shoulder, smiling wildly with a sense of triumph.

92

'Now. That's the first step. Let's figure out what to do next, Brian.'

Brian Tyson looked down at the dangling chain, looked into Squeaky's hopeful blue eyes. 'It's no use,' he told her. 'There's nowhere to run.'

'He's right, you know,' Marshal John Macafee said from the doorway. How long he had been standing there, they could not tell, but he was there now – tall, competent and just a little weary himself. He crossed to the stove, spooned out some of the vegetable stew from the iron pot and poured himself half a cup of bitter coffee.

Crossing the room, bootheels clicking on the wooden floor, he seated himself on the long bench and began to eat. Squeaky watched him with ill-concealed venom as she held Brian Tyson's head to her breast. After a few long minutes of hasty eating, Macafee returned to the stove, placed down his bowl and coffee cup and went out to stand watch in the Comanche night. He had not bothered to reaffix the shackles; he knew as well as they did that it was pointless. If any of them survived this night, it would be a miracle.

Cameron Black found the small pile of blue clothing heaped carelessly beside a clump of creosote brush. Hazzard and Jason had taken the time to shed their uniforms. They couldn't risk running into another army patrol out here wearing their blues. They must have had other clothes with them when they fled. Black didn't like Hazzard, but the man was showing that he had some animal cunning.

By starlight the going was slow, but Cameron could tell by the length of the strides of the horses he was pursuing that the deserters were no longer racing toward freedom. Maybe, symbolically, once they had shed their uniforms it seemed to them that they had made their escape. Besides, how could they know that he was riding their backtrail? Who was there remaining to leave the fort and track them down, and why would anyone be insane enough to attempt it across this renegade-infested desert?

Insane. Maybe he was, Cameron reflected; judging from the way he had conducted his life, it was a possibility he had not considered before, but perhaps he was. A reasonable man, now through enemy lines, would simply turn his pony away from more trouble, beeline it toward the safety of the nearest settlement.

What did he care about the army's problems? So

what if Young had to explain about the lost payroll? What did he care, in fact, about the people stranded there – except for Virginia they were total strangers to him. Well, Lacey and Douglas were not total strangers, but he couldn't have cared less if he found out that some renegade had lifted their scalps.

After all, the bounty hunters were after his own scalp.

Cameron did have a conscience, but what did he have to feel guilty about? Nothing, nothing at all. None of this was his doing. He was only accidentally involved. . . .

Yet he continued on, urging the gray to quicken its pace, tracking the deserters across the night-shadowed desert.

'I don't like this,' Douglas said in a dry voice. They had paused briefly by the pile of abandoned clothes to take a sip of tepid water from their canteen.

'You'll like it when it's done,' Lacey said calmly. He sat leaning forward in the saddle, his hands crossed on the pommel as the horses blew.

'He's got too much horse under him,' Douglas complained, patting the neck of his tired dun pony. 'And it's rested.'

'This isn't a race,' Lacey said to his young companion. He corked the canteen roughly with the heel of his hand and looped the straps around his saddlehorn. 'When Black does catch up with them, there'll be a fight – that much is certain. The soldiers aren't going to give up the payroll easily. We'll be there waiting when it's played out. And there will be fewer of them to deal with, you can mark my words. Be patient, Douglas. We're playing this right, I promise you.'

Douglas removed his hat and wiped his brow. He was perspiring despite the chill of the desert night. He had begun this trek as a man hoping to make a little money honorably, perhaps even riding back to Victorville to a hero's welcome after they captured Cameron Black. Now they had become something else entirely. Thieves and jackals. The feeling was unsettling. Nevertheless they had settled on this plan. Lacey had not forced him to come along.

He followed on without further complaint as Lacey tracked the horsemen ahead of them across the red sand desert by starlight.

Sometime after midnight the half-moon appeared again, lifting itself from below the horizon where a long range of serrated hills darkened the land. Cameron Black winced. The moon would make the tracking easier, but it would also offer the men he tracked a better glimpse of him. The silver sheen of the rising moon was excessively bright in comparison to the former inky, star-cluttered dead of night.

By its light Cameron saw to the south, a small collection of adobe buildings, and he wondered if Hazzard would decide to ride into the settlement, but the horses he had been following continued to line out northward, toward Santa Fe, many miles distant. That, certainly, was the destination he had in mind, and Hazzard was not willing to slow or risk being caught by an army patrol after he had gotten this far.

Walking the gray horse, at times lifting it to an easy gallop, Cameron Black rode on through the night. The moon was already riding high when he drew up with a sharp unspoken curse. From the ridge of a low outcropping he could look down into the moon-shadowed ravine below, and there he saw unmistakably the silhouettes of two horses. What man of experience camps low, he wondered? It could, of course, have been Comanches, but he doubted it, and walking his horse carefully down the slope so that its steel-shod hoofs didn't racket on the shale underfoot, he knew suddenly that he had found his men.

The faint, soft wind of the gentle night carried a distinctive odor with it. One more sign that these were not experienced trailsmen. The scent of black tobacco drifted toward him from the camp which was a good quarter of a mile away. Men don't realize how far scent travels, especially if the tracker is a man unused to partaking of what makes the smell. Coffee, tobacco, whiskey – these all had distinctive scents. Any Indian would have found this camp by smell alone. No fire was needed to mark the camp of the deserters.

His quarry rested below, believing themselves hidden in the shadows of the night when they might as well have been flying banners to announce their presence.

Cameron paused briefly, only to decide if he should proceed further mounted, or slip in to the arroyo on foot.

Finally, reluctantly, he determined that his chances of approaching unseen were better on foot; he ground-hitched the gray, placed his hat on the pommel of his saddle and, drawing his right-hand gun, crept over the rim of the arroyo and made his way toward the camp, following his night instincts. The arroyo was as dark as a tomb, the night sounds no louder than the whispering of ghosts. It was a lifeless place, a lifeless night and soon it would be filled with the confused war cries of death.

SEVEN

A horned owl swooped low on broad wings, the flapping sounds ominous in the night. A round rock skittered from beneath Cameron Black's boot and rolled into the arroyo, and he cursed silently, solemnly. Moonlight sketched his shadow before him as he moved forward in a low s crouch, his teeth clenched. One of the deserter's horses lifted its head and whickered questioningly, but the men below were not roused. Perhaps they slept, perhaps they considered themselves far from danger and were calmly smoking, mentally counting the dollars they had stolen and the pleasures the money could purchase in Santa Fe.

They were never going to make it that far.

Above and behind him, Cameron thought that he had heard other, unnatural, sounds, but convinced himself that there could be no one there. Nevertheless, he waited, watching for long minutes before, reassured by the silence of the night, he started again down the canyon flank.

Easing his way downward, another rock rolled from beneath his boot followed by a thin shower of sand. He froze his motion, but heard no reaction from the men camped below. They were either too inattentive or exhausted to notice the small sounds. Reaching the floor of the arroyo, Cameron made his way ahead noiselessly across the deep sand. To his right mesquite flourished. Beyond them was a rising, sheer, stony bluff.

He was nearly into their camp before he saw it in the darkness, and when he did he halted quickly and eased to the side, toward the screen of mesquite. Hazzard was seated on his bedroll, his back to Cameron. Jason seemed to be sleeping. Black looked skyward, took a deep breath and cocked his Colt, muffling the sound with his free hand. He stepped forward. Hazzard either heard him or saw him from the corner of his eye. He jumped up, pawing at his holster.

'Stand where you are, Hazzard. No one has to die here!'

It did nothing to stop the desperate man. He

valued the army payroll as much as he did his own life. Stumbling back, Hazzard drew his pistol, tripped over his sleeping companion and fell, his pistol discharging into the air. The racket was terrible in the close confines of the canyon, the fire from the muzzle of his Colt brilliant against the darkness. The deserters' horses, panicked by the gunshot, tossed their ground-hitches and stampeded up the canyon. Propping himself up in a seated position, Hazzard steadied his gun for a second shot.

Cameron Black was first to pull the trigger. Hazzard looked dumbly at his pistol, ferociously at Black and sagged down to die in this lonely desert dry wash.

Black strode forward. The bald-headed deserter, Jason, had risen from his bed. He had slept with his pistol near at hand, of course, and now he began to raise it, hesitated and made his offer:

'We can split the payroll, Black. Fifty-fifty.'

'Or,' Cameron suggested, 'you can get on your horse and ride off, leaving the money behind. I'll trade your life for the payroll.'

'You aren't that good,' Jason said, with a strangled laugh that was pure bluff.

'That's my last offer,' Cameron said from the

shadows. Jason hesitated. Hazzard may have valued the payroll more than his life, but Jason was a more practical man.

'We could. . . .' he began but he was interrupted by the sounds of hard-charging horses, pounding up the arroyo toward the camp. Jason muttered a curse and fired, not at Cameron Black, but at the onrushing horsemen. Cameron threw himself to the ground and rolled aside. Coming prone, he saw that the riders were not Comanche. One of them had been hit badly by Jason's shot. The other man – Black could now see clearly that it was Lacey – returned fire and Jason was spun around. With a howl of pain he dropped his weapon and started slapping at his chest where a crimson stain was spreading across his white shirt. Black fired. It was a difficult shot, firing upward from the ground at a mounted man as he pounded through the camp, and Cameron tagged nothing but sky.

Douglas trailed, his horse panicked, shying violently. As Black watched, Douglas fell from the dun's back to lay sprawled nearly on top of Hazzard. Lacey had not slowed his pony and was now far down the arroyo, around a bend in the watercourse.

Black hesitated. Perhaps, he thought, he had

managed to wing Lacey after all, but he knew his own shooting, knew that he had missed his mark. Now he rose to his knees, his eyes on the dark turn in the arroyo, got to his feet and backed into the stand of thorny mesquite, awaiting Lacey's return. For he would be back. He had to return. Too much was at stake, He had not ridden this far into the wild country to leave his task undone.

At the moment, however, there was only silence. Nothing moved in the night. The moon, riding higher, showed one flank of the arroyo plainly, while the other remained in inky darkness. If Lacey came back now, he would likely try it on foot. Cameron didn't think the man had enough Indian in him to creep up undetected, but his horse would be even a larger target. Now that Cameron knew he was there, it would not be easy to come up on him unseen. Lacey must have been thinking these same thoughts, trying to figure out a way to do it now that he had lost both the element of surprise and strength of numbers.

Cameron spotted the canvas saddle-bags containing the payroll easily enough; Hazzard and Jason had kept them near at hand.

Easing that way, Cameron snatched up the bags and shouldered them, his eyes fixed on the bend in the arroyo, his Colt cocked and ready. Then he turned and started back the way he had come, making the rugged ascent to where he had left the gray horse standing in the moonlight. Breathing hard with the exertion, Cameron stood looking downward, searching with his eyes for Lacey. Where had the bounty hunter gone? Had it been an Indian, or a man familiar with the area, Cameron would have been more concerned, thinking that there might be another trail up out of the arroyo by which he could be cut off. But he doubted that a stranger to the desert could find such a hidden trail in the night, or have knowledge of where it might lead.

Lacey was just gone! Cameron did not think the man was cowering in some nook afraid to show himself for fear of Black's guns. Lacey might be many things, but he hadn't shown himself to he a coward. The man would have a plan; he would return sooner or later.

Cameron hoisted the canvas army saddle-bags and tied them on over his own. The bags were not heavy, most of the payroll being in paper money. Swinging into leather, Cameron again paused to study the arroyo bottom, but he saw no sign of life there, only the bodies of three men dead by their own obsession over that printed paper.

He turned the gray eastward.

He did consider as he rode. There was that little collection of adobe houses he had seen earlier, but riding into an unfamiliar town with thousands of dollars, did not seem like the wisest thing to do. There was Santa Fe, of course. The way north would be clear of hostiles due to the army presence in and around the town. The Mexican border was also not that far away. A man could make it if he was cautious; there was enough money in those bags to let a man live his life out in comfort.

Cameron rode on toward the fort, his sense of righteousness barely outweighing the idea that he must be the fool of all time.

He would have to ride *back through* the enemy lines, praying that the clans had not gathered there, reinforcing the renegades, then face Young – what if Mattie had died in his absence? And, since he was still a wanted man, and Macafee knew it, take the risk that the marshal would not decide to throw an extra set of shackles on Black and take him along to face the law. Assuming any of them managed to make it out alive.

And why, for God's sake, was he still thinking about Virginia! Ginnie. So many years had passed since he had met the fresh-faced pretty girl with the raven-black hair and gentle manner. *This* Virginia Scopes he did not even know. But when he looked into her eyes, it seemed like they were young again. Maybe he did not need Virginia for herself, but to convince himself that he was still that swaggering young man he had once been.

He rode on steadily, his eyes always on the back-trail, watching for Lacey. He neared the outpost, increasingly aware that the renegades were still prowling and they would not let him pass willingly.

There are innumerable ways for a man to make a fool of himself.

'You!' Lieutenant Young said, in a voice that carried a tone of weary authority. Brian Tyson lifted his head from his arms. Squeaky, who had been sleeping in the corner beside a disconsolate Kate, also lifted her head.

'Sir?' Brian replied distantly.

'We need you.'

'You need me,' Brian repeated dully. 'For what?'

'There's only the marshal and myself to stand watch. Neither of us can make it through another night. You can shoot. I want you on the ramparts.'

'What's Macafee have to say about that – giving

me a gun?' Brian asked. Squeaky, in her camisole, had risen now, her eyes interested.

'It doesn't matter what he says. We are on an army post,' Young answered, 'but as a matter of fact he raised no objection.'

'Why should I—'

'Why! To protect your own miserable life,' Young said fiercely, 'and the lives of these young women . . . if you care about them. If you try to run, I shall personally shoot you down, Tyson. But if you perform your duty as requested, I will write a letter to whatever jury and judge you might face expressing the army's thanks. That, of course, may or may not be enough to ameliorate your sentence, but then again, it might just be enough to save you from the hangman's noose.'

'I don't—'

Squeaky spoke up: 'Oh, do it, Brian! It's at least a chance, don't you see?'

'I'll do it,' Tyson said, keeping his eyes fixed on Squeaky's hopeful face. 'Not for me, but for you. I wouldn't let any harm come to you.' Turning to Lieutenant Young he held up his manacled wrist. 'What about these?'

Young seemed to hesitate. His eyes were red, his face haggard. Finally, wondering if he was making yet another mistake, he fished a key from his trouser pocket and tossed it to Squeaky. 'You take care of that.' His last glance as he traipsed out of the ballroom held a clear warning to Brian Tyson.

On the ramparts Brian came face to face with Macafee. The unhappy lawman shoved a Springfield rifle at him and, with reluctance, a handful of cartridges.

'I want to thank you. . . .' Brian began hesitantly.

'Don't thank me. It wasn't my idea. It's a matter of necessity, that's all. Everyone's run off. We've got three men left to hold the outpost. The lieutenant's gone to his quarters to sleep. In four hours he'll be back to take my place, then it'll be your turn.' Macafee studied Brian closely as the prisoner checked the load in his weapon. 'Don't make a mistake, son,' he warned Brian. 'You can't escape anyway.'

'I don't mean to try it,' Brian said looking past the sharpened stakes of the palisade toward the moonlit desert beyond. 'I came up here, as you said, because it's a matter of necessity.'

Macafee nodded with dour satisfaction and moved down the rampart away from him. The night remained cold and silent. The Indians would be talking now, knowing that this might be their last chance to storm the fort and break into the armory. Perhaps they had been waiting to gather strength; perhaps by now they did have enough warriors, enough guns to make their try. It would still not be easy, across open ground by moonlight, but if they had sufficient numbers, they would be successful in the end. There was no way to watch the approaches on all sides. Even now the renegades might have dispersed and repositioned themselves away from the woods where they had first encamped.

There was nothing to do but wait, watch and hope.

Cameron Black pushed the big gray horse onward. The darting shadow cast by a coyote almost caused him to draw his gun, but he recognized the slinking animal for what it was in time. He knew that he dared not fire a weapon now, not this close to the fort which was ringed by renegades. His only chance was to approach as stealthily as possible and then spur the horse into a run at the last moment . . . assuming the place had not already been taken.

Cameron thought of that, but he believed he would have heard gunfire, possibly seen smoke and flames if the battle had been joined. He thought he still had time.

Another shadow leaped up from the darkness, but this was no four-legged predator. There was the impact of a human body against the side of his horse, and a hand clawed at the reins, trying to wrest them from Cameron's hands. Cameron kicked out savagely with his boot and the Indian fell back with a grunt.

He was quickly to his feet again, launching himself at Cameron as the horse circled hesitantly. Black felt a hand grip his collar, saw the silver arc of a knife flashing in the moonlight and he kicked free of the gray, rolling to the far side of the horse as the Comanche waited, hovering over him with the ten-inch long knife.

Black was quickly to his feet, his right-side Colt drawn, but he hesitated to fire still, not knowing how many others the shot might summon. The Indian, initially balked by the sight of the Colt, now circled slowly, knife held low. Perhaps he understood the situation; perhaps he believed the gun to be empty, a hollow threat. No matter, he was determined to take the big gray horse and Black's weapons.

The two faced off for long moments before,

without uttering a cry, the Comanche lunged, knife slashing at Cameron's belly. Black side-stepped, managed to trip the onrushing renegade and club down with the barrel of his Colt, stunning the Indian momentarily.

It was a glancing blow, however, and not enough to keep him down. On hands and knees the Comanche turned toward Black and started to rise. Cameron knew that now was the time to end it, before the Indian was upright and fully alert and he launched himself at the warrior.

The Comanche went to his back and raised his knees, catching Black in his wind and forcing him aside with a grunt. Still groggy, the Indian flung himself on Black, his knife raised high. Cameron caught the knife hand at the wrist and held it away from his throat, but now the weakness in his left arm, the one that had been wounded in that Alamogordo shoot-out, came into play. He could not overpower the man, bring his left hand firmly up to bend the Comanche's hand back on itself and force him to drop the knife. There was noth-ing, however, the matter with his knee, and he brought it up with savage desperation, catching his attacker between the legs and the Indian groaned and rolled half-aside.

The night was silent. No curses or war cries had been exchanged during the entire fight. There were only the effortful grunts, the panting of breath, the thud of fists meeting flesh. It was a silent duel to the death.

As the Indian relaxed ever so slightly due to the pain washing over him, Cameron switched his grip and brought the heel of his right hand up under the Comanche's jaw with all of the strength he possessed. A portion of the renegade's tongue was bitten off and blood flowed freely from his mouth. Stunned again, he went briefly slack, and Cameron Black rolled from under him and got to his feet. He hovered over the Comanche, panting, his arms hanging loosely. The renegade made to rise once more, and Cameron Black kicked him in the throat.

The attacker sagged back against the cold desert sand, his hand open, the knife gleaming brightly in the moonlight. Cameron bent, picked it up and hurled it as far as he could. Bent half-double, fighting for breath, he staggered back to where the confused gray horse waited, reins dangling, and climbed aboard. There might have been other renegades around.

It seemed unlikely. Cameron thought that this

man was yet another reservation jumper who had broken free and was attempting to join up with a larger band. Nevertheless, he rode on more cautiously than before, wary of each shadow.

He was still breathing hard; his chest and shoulder ached. The fight had taken much out of him and he made a decision:

'I'm too old for this. To hell with caution; I'm just shooting the next one who tries it.'

EIGHT

'Rider coming in!' Brian Tyson shouted. Lieutenant Young had replaced Macafee at his post and the officer leaped to the parapet in time to see the woods beyond erupt with scattered gunfire and two Indians riding their ponies bareback, whooping as they came, trying to catch a lone white man. He rode a big gray horse, obviously tiring, and leaned low across the withers, firing back with his revolver.

'I'll be damned,' Young said. 'It's Black! Let's give him some covering fire, Tyson.'

Both men opened up with their Springfields, giving the pursuing renegades something to think about. No one seemed to be hit by the gunfire, but the Comanches didn't like the feeling of being exposed to riflemen on the moon-bright flat, and they hesitated and then turned away.

Macafee, roused from his sleep shouted up, 'What the hell's going on? Are they attacking!'

'Swing the gates! It's Black coming in,' Young called back.

The marshal dropped the bar and opened the double gates wide enough for Cameron Black to ride through then quickly barred them again.

'Well, I'm damned,' Macafee said, as Black swung out of leather. 'I would have bet you wouldn't be back.'

Cameron didn't answer. He was weary, battered, hungry and thirsty. He untied the canvas sacks from behind his saddle and stood waiting for Lieutenant Young to reach them.

'Is that. . . ?' the officer asked in astonishment. Black gave him the bags containing the payroll and turned back toward his horse.

'I've got to get some sleep,' he said.

'What about the others? Hazzard and Jason? Did you run into Lacey and Douglas?' Young asked, the canvas saddle-bags draped over his shoulder. Cameron Black looked at the officer again, gathered the gray horse's reins and walked away toward the stable without another word.

Young asked Macafee, 'What do you think

happened out there?'

'I don't think Hazzard handed the payroll over willingly,' the marshal answered. He looked toward Cameron Black who was walking heavily across the parade ground. 'He'll tell us when he's ready.'

'I suppose I'd better relieve Tyson,' Lieutenant Young said, looking to the ramparts where the prisoner strode nervously from side to side. 'Let him have a little rest.'

'He could use it,' Macafee said.

'How willing was he to stand guard?' Young asked, as the two men started that way.

'I couldn't say he was willing at all,' Macafee replied, 'but I think he took your little speech about writing a recommendation for him to heart. A desperate man will grasp at straws, as they say.'

'How has he acquitted himself?' Young asked.

'Well, he did not try to shoot me, at least,' Macafee said, before grasping a ladder rung and beginning the climb.

'He made it back,' Squeaky said to Virginia Scopes, who was only half awake, wrapped up in one of the striped Indian blankets.

'What? Who?' Virginia asked muzzily.

'Black. He came back – and I think he brought the payroll with him.'

'Was he hurt?' Virginia asked.

'Not shot, but he was walking real stiff. Kind of moving tenderly, if you know what I mean,' Squeaky said. 'Don't you want to go see him, to ask him how he is?'

'Maybe I do,' Virginia said to the young girl. 'But I don't think Cameron Black wants to see me just now.'

'But surely. . . .' Squeaky began, but just then the door to the ballroom opened again and Brian Tyson, looking weary and battered himself, came in, a weak smile on his lips as he looked for and found Squeaky. The blonde rose from beside Virginia and rushed to the young prisoner, throwing her arms around his waist. They exchanged quick, muted words and walked to the long bench along the north wall. Virginia rubbed at her weary eyes and shook her head. She considered Squeaky's suggestion seriously for a few minutes and then shook her head again.

No.

She and Cam were not so young as Squeaky and her man. Their meeting were always shaded by the clouded memories of days gone past, of long years of misunderstandings. Virginia wished she could talk to Cameron Black, considered it again and

118

again rejected the notion. She rolled up once more in the mound of Indian blankets. But she could not fall asleep.

Kate, sleeping nearby, had awakened although she had not moved. As Virginia tossed in her blankets, the dark-eyed woman said to her, 'Do you know what I advised Squeaky? I told her not to let them take her young man away from her.'

Virginia did not answer.

Nor did she sleep.

Dawn was a replica of the previous morning, the duplicate of a thousand other desert dawns. The brief flash of pinkish red above the mountains, fading quickly, followed by the white light of the cloudless sky.

No one slept as dawn broke except Squeaky and Brian Tyson, bundled on the floor in one corner of the ballroom. Virginia noticed their faces, saw that they seemed totally at peace. In sleep the lines of concern had vanished from Tyson's face, leaving him looking as he was – only a lonely child to whom the even younger Squeaky now played mother. It was touching and sad at once. Even if they managed to hold off the hostiles, the young man was destined for hanging in Socorro. For now, Virginia thought, let them have their small comfort and the peace of sleep.

Kate had risen early, shed a few angry tears over the murdered Aaron Harding, straightened herself, dressed in her badly wrinkled red silk dress and prodded the fire in the potbelly stove to life. Virginia went that way.

'Well there's enough coffee for another day,' Kate said. She nodded toward the iron pot sitting on the stove. 'I wouldn't try the vegetable stew, though.'

'No,' Virginia replied, 'I wouldn't eat anything nine days old. There must be some food here. I'll have to ask Young where the larder is. A sack of cornmeal would do. Right now I wouldn't turn up my nose at mush.' The two women briefly let their eyes meet, and both laughed out loud at the memories of nights spent with the high-rollers and swells in Santa Fe when the men had treated them nightly to filet mignon and the finest wines available.

'We sure have come down,' Virginia commented, still smiling.

'Yes, we have.' Kate became serious. 'But just for a little while, Virginia, I thought I had found a new man, a new life that made all of that totally unimportant.'

Virginia turned away from the conversation as the door opened again.

Cameron Black, silhouetted by the dawn light, entered, hat in hand. He crossed the room heavily, his joints obviously stiff. His hair had been slicked back as if he had doused his head under a pump and combed it back with his fingers, which undoubtedly was what he had done. His white shirt was out at one elbow, the right knee of his jeans was similarly split. He still had not managed to shave. His boots were badly scuffed.

Virginia thought what a far cry Cameron was from the cocky young gunfighter who had worn black silk shirts, red kerchiefs and a silver armband over strong young biceps. Well, she thought, what could you expect? She was happy that there was no mirror handy for her to view herself in.

There was a distinctive smell about Cameron as he walked stiffly toward the stove. Virginia knew what it was – gun oil. She had only to glance at Cameron's twin Colts to know that he had cleaned and oiled them both that morning, caring for them like a lover. He would never neglect them; they were the one thing he would never let go.

'Any coffee left?' Cam asked.

'A little,' Virginia said. She noticed that Kate

had sidled away in case she and Cameron Black had something personal to talk about. What could there be left to talk about?

Cameron looked with distaste at the soggy remnants of the stew and said, 'Someone ought to dump that before we all get poisoned.'

'We're working on it,' Virginia said, handing Cam a cup of the strong coffee. 'How's corn meal mush sound to you?'

'Right now,' he flashed one of his infrequent grins, 'I'd trade a month's pay for some.'

Virginia smiled uneasily. They both knew that Cameron Black didn't work by the month, but rather by the job – meaning by how many men he had managed to outgun. Cameron might have been reading her thoughts. His grin fell away. Looking toward the corner of the room, he told Virginia, 'Someone is going to have to roust the kid. We need to relieve Macafee and Lieutenant Young.'

His eyes were half-averted as he asked, 'How is Mattie doing?'

'Not much better. We have to find some way to feed the baby, Cam, or he won't make it either. If we only had a cow, even a goat—'

'We don't!' Cameron Black said, much more

sharply than he intended. Virginia knew that he was as concerned, if not more so, than she. 'Feed it mush,' he added, with what was meant to be a bitter joke. Virginia took his arm as he turned away.

'Cam – how much longer will this go on? How much longer can it?'

'I don't know.' His calloused hand briefly rested on hers. 'If Colonel Hayes doesn't return soon, I'm afraid. . . .'

'Did you say something about Colonel Hayes?' Kate asked hopefully. Cameron lied to her.

'I said that I'm sure he'll be returning soon.'

He caught Virginia's eyes again briefly, half-smiled and strode to the corner, tin cup of coffee in hand to rouse Brian Tyson for guard duty.

Black once more climbed to the ramparts. Lieutenant Young watched his arrival with dead eyes. He rose from the bench and told Black, 'They've been moving around, and it seems that there's quite a few more now.'

Black checked the loads in his Winchester and replied, 'We'll keep a sharp eye out. I don't think they will hold back much longer.'

'No, I don't think so either. They've been keeping a close enough eye on us to know our strength.

They can't risk Colonel Hayes and the company returning, not if they want a chance at the armory.'

All the while that the lieutenant was speaking, Cameron sensed that his mind was somewhere else. They faced a life and death struggle, hut the lieutenant's mind was fixed on a more personal life-or-death situation. He said softly, 'She'll be all right, sir.'

The lieutenant nodded; his face was expressionless. 'Where's Tyson?'

'He'll be along. He stopped for one cup of coffee, that's all.'

'Black,' the lieutenant said, as he turned halfaway, 'I don't mean to seem weak. I'm just . . . so tired.' He straightened up and said in a firmer voice, 'Call me if they attack.'

'You'll hear it, sir.'

'I wish everyone had a Winchester repeater,' he said, nodding at Cameron's gun. 'Then even four of us could hold back a few dozen raiders, couldn't we?'

Cameron didn't answer. Wishing did no good. They didn't have the newer weapons, and that was that. Black always carried the best weapons available: they were his lifeblood. Why the army did not was a mystery. He watched as Young made his way toward the ladder, seemingly a beaten man.

'Where's the kid?' Marshal Macafee said, striding toward Black. Cameron repeated what he had told Young. 'Did the lieutenant tell you? – we saw a lot of movement out there just before dawn. It seems they're going to try to circle the place.'

'He told me,' Black said woodenly. His attention was not on the marshal, but on the copse where they knew the main body of Indians sheltered. The cottonwood trees there trembled in the morning breeze. No shadow resembling a man could be made out over the distance.

Still it felt as if. . . .

Cameron turned his head at the sound of approaching boots. Brian Tyson was clambering up the ladder, his pale face uncertain, his mouth set unhappily.

'Made it, did you?' Macafee said, as Brian achieved the planks of the parapet.

'Yes . . . you get down!' Brian yelled, and he pushed Macafee aside, went to one knee and fired his rifle as Cameron stood unmoving, taken by surprise. Then he too saw the target. An Indian had somehow scaled the western face of the fort and had been leveling his musket sights on Macafee's back. Brian's shot took the Comanche full in the chest and he fell silently away.

'How the hell did he. . . ?' Macafee asked, panting as he sat down. Cameron Black, rifle cocked and ready, rushed that way to find out.

'Any more of them?' Tyson asked, reloading his Springfield. The kid looked excited but not frightened. Perhaps his nearness to death shielded him from panic.

'That's all,' Cameron called back. Somehow in the night the Indians had managed to prop a dead tree up against the side of the fort and this one warrior, more agile or daring than the others had scaled it, seeking to count coup. The dead man lay twisted and broken against the sand below.

'That happened on my watch,' Macafee said, rubbing his forehead like a man in agony. 'One man made it up. It could have been a dozen. I wonder if I fell asleep! I'm just tired, so damned tired.'

'We're all tired,' Black said, briefly resting his hand on John Macafee's shoulder. 'These interminable watches are getting to us. Any one of us could have been standing guard when it happened.'

'I am just . . . so damned tired,' Macafee said again. Only now did the veteran lawman seem to be showing his age.

'Get some sleep,' Cameron advised.

'Yes, that's all I need,' Macafee replied. He looked at Brian Tyson and said, 'Thanks for saving my life, kid. I might he getting old but there are still a few things I'd like to have the chance of doing before I go.'

Brian shrugged and muttered uncomfortably, 'We're all in this together, Marshal.'

The old lawman again murmured his thanks and made his way heavily to the ladder and back down to the ground.

At least, Cameron thought, they now knew what the renegades had been up to the night before. Young and Macafee had been alert enough to figure that something was up, but not sharp enough to discover what it was. Lucky for all of them that climbing the dead tree in the middle of the night had proven too formidable for the Comanches. If they had managed to clamber up. . . .

'Shoot at anything that moves,' Cameron Black advised Brian. '*Anything.* The only thing we are not short of is ammunition. No sense hesitating.'

Brian nodded although the idea went against everything he had ever been taught about weapons. The first rule was to know your target before you fired. In their present situation common sense trumped wisdom.

For the hell of it, Cameron Black fired five carefully spaced shots into the woods beyond the desert flats. As he had told Brian, running out of ammunition was not their primary concern, and it was surprising how a few lead slugs flying past will give a man cause to seriously consider matters before lifting his head.

'Let them have a couple from time to time,' Cameron said, jacking the last exploded cartridge from his Winchester to join the group of bright brass casings at his feet.

Brian nodded although shooting at nothing was in direct contradiction to his upbringing. When he was a boy, ammunition was dear and his father had counted out the bullets his sons were allowed for each day's hunting, and for each expended round, Dad expected there to he a game animal brought home.

'That girl!' Cameron called out unexpectedly. Brian was well along the parapet and his head came around curiously. 'Squeaky! I've been wondering, what's her real name, Brian?'

'You know what, Black,' Brian Tyson called back,

'I don't know. And to tell you the truth, I could not care less!'

Cameron grinned inwardly. Yes, that was what it was like to be young. At times he forgot.

'What do you call *her*?' Brian asked Cameron.

'Who do you mean?'

'Virginia Scopes. The one you keep sliding glances off of.'

'Ginnie,' Cameron called back. *I call her Ginnie. I always have.*

'Look out!' Brian Tyson hollered. 'Here comes trouble!'

NINE

Cameron Black spun around, jacking a fresh cartridge into the receiver of his Winchester. What he saw as he looked out across the desert was not what he had imagined, no wild surging charge of Comanche renegades, but a lone white man trying to stay in the saddle as he flagged a foundering dun horse onward toward the fort.

It was the bounty hunter, Lacey.

'What do we do, Cameron?' Brian asked, having eased closer.

'I'd as soon let the renegades have him, but I suppose you'd better scramble down and open the gate. I'll watch his back in case they decide to go for him.' That seemed unlikely. The Comanches knew that they would have to enter the field of fire in broad daylight and the dun horse was hardly a prize worth dying for; Lacey had run the animal half to death.

Once the gates were barred behind Lacey, Cameron slipped down to join the others. It could be that Lacey could provide some new information about the Comanche forces. The dun horse stood heaving and shuddering. It was obviously foundering. Lacey seemed oblivious of the animal's suffering. He turned his full fury on Cameron Black.

'So, you did get hack!' Lacey panted. 'Did you tell the lieutenant what you did with the payroll?'

'I've got it locked up again, Lacey,' Young told him.

'You . . .' Lacey seemed slightly deflated. 'That's all to the good,' he said, removing his hat to wipe back his hair as he leaned against the unsteady dun horse. 'But did he tell you how he recovered it? He shot three men down.'

Cameron Black's eyes steeled. 'I can't abide a liar, Lacey. The truth is that you shot those men down in their beds, and you know it.'

'I did not! And I am not on trial here,' Lacey protested vigorously.

'Nor am I,' Cameron Black said coldly, and he

turned his back to walk away.

'This isn't over, Black!' Lacey swore, 'Victorville sent us out to capture you, and as far as I'm concerned you are my prisoner.' He looked fussily to Young and Macafee, but the response he got was not what he hoped for. Macafee simply shrugged and walked away toward the ladder.

Lieutenant Young said, 'That horse might still be saved if you cool him down properly.'

'The hell with the horse!' Lacey shouted, his eyes still fixed on Cameron's back. 'What do I care about that piece of dog's meat?'

'Maybe not much now,' Young replied, 'but if there comes the day when you find yourself trying to walk back to Victorville, you might find that it is worth a lot to you.' Then Young's focus was shifted as from the BOQ, the mewling sound of a suffering infant rose. He too walked deliberately away from Lacey, leaving the bounty hunter utterly frustrated. Lacey loosened the cinches on the dun pony with shaking hands and walked it up and down, trying to cool the animal before leading it to water and feed.

Brian Tyson, holding the fort alone, watched as Macafee climbed up to join him. 'I saw all of that,'

Brian said. 'The man just won't quit, will he?'

'Lacey went out after the payroll,' Macafee said thoughtfully, watching the open ground before the outpost as he spoke. 'No one believes otherwise. Whatever happened out there, Black brought the money back. Now he's trying to salvage some self-respect and at least end up with the bounty for bringing Black back to Victorville.

'No,' the marshal added more roughly, 'he won't quit. Not because he thinks he's in the right, but because he knows he's wrong.'

Brian asked hesitantly, 'But when he braces Cameron Black. . . ?'

'Then,' Macafee said definitely, 'he will quit cold.'

Brian wondered at the marshal's stance. If Black were a wanted man and Lacey an appointed law officer, why then did Macafee seem to be siding with Cameron? Perhaps the old man was not so stiff in his prejudices toward duty as Brian had believed. Perhaps it was simply, as Macafee had said, not his business, Victorville being far removed from his jurisdiction.

No matter! It affected his own situation not a whit. Brian tugged his hat lower against the harsh sunlight and paced the wall, watching for the

Comanches to make another move – and thinking of Squeaky to whom he had made the thinnest sort of promise. The sort that begins with 'If,' and ends with 'maybe'. His thoughts snarled and tangled on themselves so that he found himself actually wishing that the Indians would attack. *That* at least was something he could do something about. But they did not make their move, did not stir as the naked sun rose higher, turning the desert into a blast furnace. He and Macafee shared the ramparts in uneasy silence.

'No change?' Lieutenant Young asked Virginia. Mattie still lay as in death on the white sheets of her bed, her face waxen and too-still. The baby, on the other hand, alternately squalled, clenched tiny hands, twisted its head from side to side searching for nourishment at Virginia's breast.

'Mattie's been though hell; she'll need a lot of time to mend. The baby,' Virginia said, 'must have milk soon. If we had a cow. . . .'

'We have none,' Young said. He sat beside Mattie, his face a mask of anguish. 'If we'd had a decent surgeon. . . .'

'You had a man who did his best under difficult circumstances.' Victoria told him, sensing that the young officer was angry with Cameron Black for circumstances beyond his control. 'If not for him, you wouldn't even have had a live-born son. Think of the babe as well, Young! He, we can do something to help. No one knows if Mattie will get well. You have to hope for the best and plan for the worst.'

She was silent, petting the newborn infant's reddish head where sparse black hair grew in fuzzy clusters. 'Cameron said that the Indians sometimes resort to mare's milk when the mother cannot nurse and there is no wet-nurse in the camp,' Virginia said quietly.

Lieutenant Young rose, tugged the skirts of his tunic down and said coldly, 'Cameron Black must also know that the US Army does not utilize mares.' He paused and added bitterly, 'They are nothing but trouble.'

With that he went out again, leaving the door open to the harsh sunlight and dry heat. Baby in her arms, Virginia rose to close the door after him. She pitied the officer, but she was beginning to lose patience with him. Sorrow for his wife was understandable, but his seeming indifference toward his new son was not. Sagging back into the chair, Virginia opened the blanket covering the new infant a little further and asked it, 'Well, maybe Cameron is right. Do you think you'd like to at least try some corn meal mush mashed up fine?'

Cameron Black found that there was still coffee in the ballroom. He poured a tepid cup of the stuff, trying to remember the last time he had eaten a full meal. There was mush simmering in the big iron pot. Kate stood over it, stirring it with a wooden spoon. Her domestic posture was at odds with the red silk dress she wore. Her eyes were distant and damp, perhaps still remembering Aaron Harding.

'Have some?' she asked with a weak smile.

'I suppose so. I used to like that with a lot of butter, brown sugar or syrup.'

'Well,' Kate said, 'I found some salt. There's that. Nothing more.'

Cameron shrugged, the mush would at least sustain life a little longer.

Kate asked, 'The killers. The men who shot Aaron down . . . they won't be coming back, will they?'

'No,' Cameron answered, understanding her question.

'Good!' she said, spooning a huge dollop of mush into a blue ceramic bowl.

Cameron left her to her sorrows and walked to the bench along the wall. It was a mad collection of men and women the outpost had collected, not a single one of them happy or with much hope for the future. Brian Tyson, Squeaky, Kate, Lieutenant Young, Manic, Virginia . . . and him. A collection of doomed souls, it seemed.

'I'll see if the baby can possibly handle this,' he heard Kate say to no one, and she went out the door with a bowl filled with finely mashed corn-meal mush. After a few minutes Virginia swept in, looking as tired as the ages, her silver-streaked dark hair loose around her shoulders. She poured a cup of coffee and sat beside Cameron Black.

'Any luck?' he asked.

'Kate's still trying, but even mashed up fine, it's no food for a newborn child.' She closed her eyes and leaned her head back wearily. 'Is it the times, Cam, or is it us?' she murmured, but he had no answer for her. He did not honestly know. His thoughts flashed briefly to the young, cocksure Cameron Black and the dark-eyed beauty he had claimed . . . the image wisped away. The past has no reality; it's no more than a dream unrealized, faded by the light of morning. He closed his own eyes, aware of the strangely comforting touch of her shoulder against his own. . . .

The barrage of shots from beyond snapped Cameron's head up. He groped for his rifle and moved past the sleep-stunned eyes of Virginia Scopes, staggering toward the door. Lieutenant Young was coming at the run, his eyes swollen, movements inexact.

'What is it?' the officer shouted. 'They can't be attacking again – not in broad daylight!'

'I don't know, but we'd better get up there,' Cameron answered, rubbing the sleep from his own eyes.

From the ramparts they could see powder-smoke. Brian Tyson and Macafee were burning some ammunition, and with deadly intent. Achieving the elevated plankwalk, Cameron yelled out, 'What's happening?' but there was no time for an answer. Across the open land before them at least two dozen renegade Comanches were attacking, all but one afoot. From the sound of the reports and the billows of smoke, Cameron knew that all were armed with primitive muzzle-loaders. Inaccurate and slow to load. That would be of little comfort to a man who was tagged by a musket ball.

Cameron Black settled down to the deadly task. His Winchester repeater was a dozen times faster than anything the Indians possessed, and far more accurate. He took down three advancing Indians with his first five shots. Beside him another repeating rifle was firing and from the corner of his eye he saw that it was Lacey who was similarly armed with a Henry repeater.

It was enough to break the spine of the renegade attack. They simply did not have the firepower to breach the outpost's defenses with their outdated weapons.

Which was the reason they had wanted to break into the armory in the first place. 'They've no chance of taking the fort,' young Brian Tyson said, reloading his Springfield.

'It's a matter of time,' Lieutenant Young responded dismally. 'Against twenty muskets we can hold our own. But what if it is fifty, or a hundred as the clan gathers? With our dwindling supplies . . . we will even be out of water in a week.'

Cameron said nothing. What he felt like doing was taking the young officer and shaking him, reminding him that he was a US Army officer and everything depended on him maintaining command. But he did not do that. The man was a wreck emotionally. Cameron doubted that anything he said would even penetrate the cocoon Young had gradually wrapped around himself.

He checked the loads in his rifle, mentally counting the boxes of shells he had in his saddle-bags. Maybe the army had enough ammunition to keep burning through the barrels of their outmoded .45–70s, but the ammunition for the Winchester was drawing down to a dangerous level. The lieutenant, unfortunately, was right.

It was just a matter of time. And they were all exhausted. Look at what had happened to Macafee, one of their most experienced fighters. The renegades had managed to throw the roughly made assault device up against the walls of the outpost the night before under his watch. It could only get worse.

Across the open area of the dusty parade ground, the struggling infant cried out again.

'I say we bust out,' Lacey was saying in the cooling ballroom. No one paid any attention to him. Such as it was, the security of the outpost was all they had. 'I mean,' he continued, speaking to no one, 'we're going to just shrivel up and die here.'

'The colonel will be back,' Lieutenant Young said as if it were an article of faith.

Brian and Macafee were again standing watch. Cameron Black and Young were drinking what seemed to be the last of the coffee while Lacey paced. The three women watched him uncertainly. The bounty hunter seemed on the brink of madness. His cocksure attitude and hopes of riches had long since faded. He was thinking now only of survival.

'He'll be back, will he?' Lacey asked wildly. 'And in the meantime – have you told these women what the renegades can do to white women?' A sweep of his hand took in Squeaky, Kate and Virginia.

'There's no way out,' Cameron Black said softly.

'You made it once, didn't you?' Lacey objected.

'A lone man on a fast horse is one thing . . . besides, there were fewer of the enemy then. They've gathered now, Lacey. It can't be done.'

'So you're willing to just wait and see what harm comes to these women!' Lacey demanded.

Cameron Black looked at the jittery Squeaky, the bone-weary Kate, at Virginia Scopes and answered, 'We're safer forted up, Lacey. Making a dash across the desert is just plain reckless.'

'We're going nowhere,' Young said definitely. They all knew what he meant. With the fastest horses, the best rifles, he could not move his wife and newborn son with any hope for their survival. He turned to Lacey. 'You, sir, are a civilian, you may do as you please.'

And then Young went out into the cold night. Cameron saw him briefly raise his arms skyward in a desperate plea.

'Black?' Lacey begged.

'Lacey,' Cameron answered, his voice as cold as ice, 'I wouldn't ride with you toward the Pearly Gates if the chasm of Hell was opening under me.'

'Well, damn you all then!' Lacey shouted. 'I'm going to make my try.'

'Good luck to you,' John Macafee said numbly, dumping the dregs of his coffee cup into the cinders of the stove where they hissed and sputtered in the slowly dying fire.

'It's all over, isn't it, Cam?' Virginia Scopes asked, as they stood outside in the faint glow of moonlight.

'Is it? I don't know. I never know when these moments come up.' He paused, looked skyward, at his boot toes and repeated, 'I just never know. I

142

suppose I'm simple-minded.'

'What are we talking about?' Virginia asked and, inexplicably she laughed out loud.

'About things being over.'

'Yes,' she said wryly, 'I got that – but what are we talking about exactly?'

Cameron Black mumbled his response. 'Bunch of renegade Indians.'

'All right,' she said, briefly touching his arm in the way she had come to adopt. 'Then is it all over?'

'Hell no!' Cameron Black said explosively. 'They can't beat me down. You know that, Ginnie!'

'I guess I do, Cam,' Virginia Scopes said, touching his arm again as he shifted his eyes down and away from her once more. 'I know that nothing can ever beat you down, Cam.'

'You'd think not, wouldn't you?' he answered sullenly before he turned away and walked toward the parapet. Virginia's only response was a throttled expulsion of breath. Then. tightening her shawl around her, she re-entered the gloomy ballroom.

The sound of furious gunfire erupted suddenly, more explosive and deadly than any they had experienced before and the men, moving with

143

haste, with the expressionless determination of the dead roused from their graves, returned to the parapets.

TEN

The Indians, many more than they had believed to be hidden in the woods, swarmed across the open ground between the copse and the outpost, the starlight striking their sketchy shadows against the dark sand.

'We'll never hold them off!' Macafee said. 'We're done this time.'

He began to fire, deliberately, emotionlessly as a man in a shooting gallery. Cameron saw at least two of the raiders go down. He himself was burning ammunition through the Winchester as rapidly as possible. It was Lieutenant Young who first comprehended what the situation was.

'Hold your fire, men!' the young officer shouted out. 'They're not attacking, they're scattering.'

And it was true, for behind the fleeing

Comanches they now saw the vanguard of the pursuing cavalry patrol. Muzzle flashes illuminated the night, powdersmoke drifted across the plains. Sabers flashed in the light of the stars.

'It's Colonel Hayes!' Young cried out with inexpressible relief choking his voice.

It was true. It seemed likely that the large body of renegades he had been following had led him to the gathered clan. Now the troopers rode the surprised enemy down and the skirmish, brief but violent, raised an incredible clamor over the desert.

The battle ended as abruptly as it had begun. The reservation jumpers did not have the heart to face a massed cavalry attack, and singly, in pairs, in small groups they fled back onto the long desert. A few escaped, but many were ridden down by the battle-hardened cavalrymen. The pale moon, when it rose, revealed dozens of inert men sprawled against the flats. For them the fight had ended.

Young clambered quickly down the ladder and flung the gates wide for the returning company of men. The horse soldiers trailed in, some laughing, some dour and disgusted, a few wounded, most only bone-weary from the long trail.

In their midst was a tall, silver-mustached man

146

whom Cameron knew had to be Hayes even before he saw the silver eagle insignia on his epaulets. His day was not ended. He shouted instruction to his NCOs concerning food, stabling, care for the wounded. It was a long while before the parade ground settled and he was able to accept Lieutenant Young's salute.

'How goes it, Young?' the colonel said in a weary voice.

'We held the fort, sir.'

'That is all that could be expected of you,' Hayes said, now sounding exhausted. 'All that was required.'

'Shall I keep my report until morning?' Young asked.

'Please. If you don't mind,' Colonel Hayes answered. 'For now, I must dismount or fall – and as much amusement as that might afford the company, I shall not allow it.' A trooper standing nearby held the bridle to the colonel's sorrel horse as he swung down stiffly. It appeared to Cameron, standing nearby, that the man had been injured, but beyond an uncomfortable grunt, the colonel gave no sign of it. He made his way slowly toward the headquarters building, pausing for a moment as Mattie's new baby cried. Then, shaking his head, the officer went into his rooms.

'So it appears that all is saved,' Lieutenant Young said with more enthusiasm than he had shown for days. 'The place isn't burned to the ground and the payroll is intact.'

'So it seems,' Cameron said grumpily. 'Your career's intact. Everything is fine.'

Young frowned, not understanding Black's dour mood, but he posed no questions. Black trod away as well, and Young busied himself trying to find four troopers who were willing to stand watch. Marshal Macafee and Brian Tyson stood facing each other on the ramparts.

'I guess it's over, then,' Tyson said, gripping his rifle tightly.

'I guess it is,' Macafee answered. Brian Tyson watched as the marshal groped for words. 'Get some rest, kid, we all need it,' was what Macafee said in the end and he climbed down the ladder to the parade ground, crossing toward the ballroom. Tyson, left alone could only stand and wonder what, if anything, the marshal's words signified.

When a trio of disgruntled, trail-dusty troopers arrived to take over the watch duty, grumbling and cursing in the time-honored manner of irritated soldiers, Brian left them to their task and scooted down the ladder himself. The outpost belonged to the army again; he had nothing more to contribute.

Crossing the packed earth of the compound, he noticed in the shadows beside the sutler's store, a figure in a red dress in close conversation with a young soldier, his cap tilted back. Brian smiled loosely. Kate had other friends, it seemed. Maybe she would forget Aaron Harding in time. Or, perhaps, by morning.

He would never forget Squeaky; he wanted her as badly as ever. He still had not asked her, however, how much she might need him. Perhaps the arrival of the troopers had changed everything. Maybe he had been – at the time – her last resort. He reflected that he knew so little about life in general and women in particular. Just a dumb kid heading for a meeting with the hangman. It had been a short, savage and sorrowful life.

Brian entered the ballroom and sat at the table, placing his rifle aside. He placed his head down on his forearms. He felt more than heard Squeaky as she slid beside him on the bench and gently touched his shoulder, saying nothing.

*

149

'You could talk to the marshal,' Virginia said to Cameron. Her eyes were fixed on Squeaky and Brian Tyson.

'And say what?' Cameron Black asked. 'It's not my business. The lieutenant told him that he'd write a letter commending his actions, didn't he? That might be enough to sway a jury.'

'To keep him from hanging, maybe,' Virginia said. 'He'll still do a lot of time, hard time in the Yuma Territorial Prison.'

'Well . . . he shouldn't have shot the man down, then.'

'He was protecting the girl, Cam! He thought his boss had given him a job to do and he was trying to do it.'

'That's what I thought I was doing,' Cameron Black said bitterly.

Virginia watched him silently, picked up one of his callused hands and whispered, 'They're just kids, Cam. Neither of them knows much.'

'Well, live and learn,' he said without looking at her.

'With any luck!' Virginia Scopes said, unexpectedly laughing. 'Do we ever, Cam? Do we ever learn much at all? Look at us!'

He did not answer and the ballroom fell silent.

The lanterns had been turned down. The weary soldiers slept deeply in the barracks. Virginia had rested her head on Cameron Black's shoulder. Macafee snored lightly. Across the room Lacey sat, eyes wide open, arms folded, staring at Cameron Black.

He's not giving up on the reward, Cameron thought. But he did close his own eyes and finally fall off to sleep with the woman-comfort of Virginia beside him. Although his hand never strayed far from his holstered Colt.

Morning was bright and dear, different from any the past few days had offered. There was the sound of a bugle and the men assembling as the flag was run up in the center of the parade ground. Across the way, from the cookhouse in the barracks, smoke rose: bacon was being fried and hotcakes flipped for hungry men. Among the confusion of the night before, they had not noticed a supply wagon roll in, but apparently one had. The soldiers were obviously weary, but pleased to be back in their regular routine, it seemed. A small contingent of men could be seen saddling near the corral, probably being dispatched to sweep the area for any remaining renegades.

151

The sky held only the haziest memory of pink. Dawn had been swept away as they slept. Cameron stood before the ballroom, watching all of the varied scenes of an army post in motion.

'You'll be riding, then?' Virginia asked at his shoulder. He turned as if surprised, but he wasn't. Not really.

'Yes. Why would I stay here?'

'Where are you going?'

'Santa Fe, I suppose.'

'What's there?' Virginia asked. Cameron Black shrugged.

'I won't know until I get there.'

'Maybe . . .' She was long silent. 'I could ride along with you. We could talk along the way.'

'Is there anything we haven't already said?'

'I guess not. It's a hard and dangerous trek for a woman alone, though, Cam. If you'd help me out. . . .'

'Sure,' he said indifferently. 'Do you have a horse?'

'The one I rode up here. There's the wagon team horses as well, but I guess I'll just leave them.'

'In an hour then,' Cameron said. 'Are we riding alone?'

'So it seems. Squeaky is determined to go along

152

with Brian to Socorro, to be with him until the bitter end.'

'What about Kate?' he inquired.

'She's decided to stay on here for awhile. There's a Corporal Clay she knows. . . .'

'She makes friends easily.'

'Kate always has,' Virginia agreed. Smiling meaninglessly, she said, 'I'd better gather up my few possessions and say goodbye to the girls. Would you saddle my horse? It's the piebald with the notched ear.'

'All right,' Cameron agreed gloomily. What was she up to now? And did it matter? Crossing the parade ground, he wove his way through blue jacketed troopers setting off on their individual assignments. He was nearly past the BOQ when he heard Lieutenant Young's familiar voice call out.

'Black!'

Now what? He halted and strode that way. Young had shaved, parted and combed his hair back. He wore a crisp new uniform and a hearty smile Black that had not seen on his face throughout the siege.

'What is it, Young?' Black asked, stepping up onto the plankwalk.

'I wanted to thank you, Black. Thank you for the miracle. Step inside for a minute.'

153

Inside the cool of the room, Cameron saw Mattie Young propped up on a few pillows. She had covered herself modestly, but it was easy to discern that beneath the sheet a young, eager babe was nursing, at peace with the world. Mattie's hair was brushed; her pale face shined with contentment. She smiled up at Cameron Black.

'Thank you,' she said. 'You can't know how much we thank you.'

Embarrassed, Cameron growled, 'Just don't call me next time.'

Then he went out again into the brilliant sunlight and found himself whistling as he crossed to the stables. Well, he thought, it goes to show you – everything can't *always* go wrong.

Finding his saddle he fixed the gray for the trail. The trooper on duty there showed him where Virginia had stored her tack and he saddled her placid-looking little piebald pony as well. Leading both out into the yard where a wood-cutting party was being assembled, axes on their shoulders, he heard a shout of warning from the ballroom porch.

'Stop that man! He's an escaped prisoner!' Lacey was bellowing, pointing a finger at the recognizable Brian Tyson and Squeaky who were riding slowly past the guards on duty. Cameron drew near enough to hear the exchange between Marshal Macafee and Lacey.

'He's getting away!' Lacey shouted.

Macafee looked toward the gate and nodded. 'Oh, well. I've had a few prisoners get away from me before, and I've still kept my job.' Then he turned and re-entered the ballroom. Lacey stood fuming, before finally he realized that it was none of his business, threw his hands skyward and followed on the heels of Macafee toward the boiling coffee pot.

Cameron remained outside, and in another minute, Virginia, carrying a red and black carpet-bag, came out into the light of day, the hood of her blue dress over her dark hair.

'Are we ready?' she asked.

'As ready as we're going to be,' Cameron answered, and he took the carpet bag from her, tying it on behind the piebald pony's saddle.

The bleary-eyed troopers on guard took only a cursory glance at them – that, presumably because of the always interesting sight of a woman – and allowed them to pass through. Cameron had felt no need to say a second goodbye to Lieutenant Young, nor to Colonel Hayes who probably had more important matters to attend to.

The desert lay long, flat and vacant as they rode. Cameron noted the fork in the trail where Squeaky and Brian Tyson had forked off toward the south and mentioned it. They both wished the young couple well, but for the most part they traveled in silence. Perhaps they *had* already said everything that could be said between them. As they traveled northward, toward Santa Fe, the land began to rise and fold somewhat, forming canyons and brush-clotted knolls. Still the desert was silent; they did not speak; the vultures in the sky made no sound as they circled lazily seeking carrion.

It was a desolate land, a desolate time, Cameron was thinking. From time to time he glanced at the unspeaking woman beside him, admiring her erect posture in the saddle, the lines and curves of her full-grown woman's body, but he did not have the urge to speak to her again.

They had traveled only ten miles when the gunman rose up out of an arroyo heavily overgrown with willow brush and manzanita and shouldered his rifle.

'Get down!' Cameron yelled at Virginia and he shoved her roughly from the saddle. He slithered his right-hand Colt from its oiled holster, but he was too slow.

A shot from Lacey's Henry rifle tagged Cameron in his shoulder and he fell numbly from the back of his gray, the pistol dropping away. He pawed at his other gun with his nearly useless left hand and rolled onto his hack as the bounty hunter charged toward him on foot, hatless, his eyes wild with triumph.

Cameron eared back the hammer of his Colt .44 and shot him full in the chest.

Lacey staggered, twisted to one side, tried to curse, tried to trigger off another round, failed in both attempts and fell dead nearly at Cameron Black's feet.

Sweat trickled into Cameron's eyes as he rolled, got slowly to hands and knees and crawled to where Ginnie lay sprawled and disoriented against the earth. Her dark blue skirt had ridden high, revealing her camisole. Her hair was covered with sand. Cameron managed to sit upright beside her, half lift her and hold her to him. Dazedly Virginia looked at him.

'Was that it, Cam? Is it over now?' she asked.

'Bastard got my right shoulder!' he replied savagely. 'Here I am now a gunhand with two crippled arms!'

Virginia, her head clearing, got to work, binding the furrow Lacey's bullet had grooved across Cameron's shoulder with cloth torn from her petticoat.

'How's it look?' he asked.

'How does it feel?' she shot back, out of frustration. She tightened the knot on the bandage. 'It looks like you couldn't outdraw a suckling infant.'

Cameron, unexpectedly, laughed out loud. Virginia realized that it was the first time in many years that she had heard the hard-bitten gunfighter laugh.

'Then, I guess I need to find a new line of work, don't I?'

Gravely he studied Virginia's intent face, 'How about you?'

'I think, Cam,' Ginnie answered quietly, 'that there is still a lot of talking we need to do along the trail.'